# GEOGRAPHY CLUB

BRENT HARTINGER

# GEOGRAPHY CLUB

HarperTempest
*An Imprint of* HarperCollins*Publishers*

Geography Club

Copyright © 2003 by Brent Hartinger

www.harperteen.com

Library of Congress Cataloging-in-Publication Data

Hartinger, Brent.

Geography Club / by Brent Hartinger.

p. cm.

Summary: A group of gay and lesbian teenagers finds mutual support when they form the "Geography Club" at their high school.

ISBN 0-06-001221-8 — ISBN 0-06-001222-6 (lib. bdg.)

[1. Homosexuality—Fiction. 2. Clubs—Fiction. 3. High schools—Fiction. 4. Schools—Fiction.] I. Title.

PZ7.H2635 Ge 2002                                        2001051736

[Fic]—dc21                                                          CIP

AC

Book design by Alison Donalty

1  3  5  7  9  10  8  6  4  2

❖

First Edition

**FOR MICHAEL JENSEN**

My own journey begins and ends with you

# GEOGRAPHY CLUB

## CHAPTER ONE

I WAS DEEP BEHIND ENEMY LINES, in the very heart of
the opposing camp. My adversaries were all around
me. For the time being, my disguise was holding, but
still I felt exposed, naked, as if my secret was obvious to
anyone who took the time to look. I knew that any
wrong action, however slight, could expose my decep-
tion and reveal my true identity. The thought made my
skin prickle. The enemy would not take kindly to my
infiltration of their ranks, especially not here, in their
inner sanctum.

Then Kevin Land leaned over the wooden bench
behind my locker and said, "Yo, Middlebrook, let me
use your shampoo!"

I was in the high school boys' locker room at the end of third period P.E. class. I'd just come from the showers, and part of the reason I felt naked was because I *was* naked. I'd slung my wet towel over the metal door of my locker and was standing there all goosebumpy, eager to get dressed and get the hell out of there. Why exactly did I feel like the boys' locker room after third period P.E. was enemy territory—that the other guys in my class were rival soldiers in some warlike struggle for domination? Well, there's not really a short answer to that question.

"Use your own damn shampoo," I said to Kevin, crouching down in front of my locker, probing the darkness for clean underwear.

Kevin stepped right up next to me and started searching the upper reaches of my locker himself. I could feel the heat of his body, but it did nothing to lessen my goosebumps. "Come on," he said. "Where is it? I know you have some. You always have shampoo, just like you always have clean undies."

I had just found my Jockey shorts, and I was tempted to not give Kevin the satisfaction of seeing he'd been right about me, but I was cold and tired of being exposed. I sat down on the bench, maneuvering my legs through the elastic of my underwear, then pulled them up. I fumbled for the shampoo in my backpack and handed it to Kevin. "Here," I said. "Just bring it back when you're done." Kevin was lean and muscled and dark, with perfect sideburns and a five o'clock shadow by ten in the morning. More important, he was naked too, and suddenly it seemed like there was no place to look in the entire locker room that wasn't his crotch. I glanced away, but there were more visual land mines to avoid—specifically, the bodies of Leon and Brad and Jarred and Ramone, other guys from our P.E. class, all looking like one of those Abercrombie & Fitch underwear ads come to life.

Okay, maybe there *was* a short answer to the question of why I felt out of place in the boys' locker room. I liked guys. Seeing them naked, I mean. But—and this is worth emphasizing—I liked seeing them naked on the Internet; I had absolutely no interest in seeing them naked, in person, in the boys' locker room after third period P.E. I'd never been naked with a guy—I mean in a sexual way—and I had no plans to do it anytime soon. But the fact that I even thought about getting naked with a guy in a sexual way was something that Kevin and Leon and Brad and Jarred and Ramone would never ever understand. I wasn't the most popular guy at Robert L. Goodkind High School, but I wasn't the least popular either. (Kevin Land at least spoke to me, even if it was only to ask for shampoo.) But one sure way to *become* the least popular guy was to have people think you might be gay. And not being gay wasn't just about not throwing a bone in the showers. It was a whole way of acting around other guys, a level of casualness, of comfort, that says, "I'm one of you. I fit in." I wasn't one of them, I didn't fit in, but they didn't need to know that.

Kevin snatched the shampoo, and I deliberately turned my back to him, stepping awkwardly into my jeans.

"Hey, Middlebrook!" Kevin said to me. "Nice ass!" Leon and Brad and Jarred and Ramone all laughed. Big joke, not exactly at my expense, but in my general vicinity. Some tiny part of me wondered, *Do* I have a nice ass? Hell, I didn't know. But a much bigger part of me tensed, because I knew this was a test, the kind enemy soldiers in movies give to the hero who they suspect isn't one of them. And from a guy I'd just lent my shampoo to, besides. So much for gratitude.

Everything now depended on my reaction. Would I pass this, Kevin Land's latest test of my manhood?

I glanced back at Kevin, who was still snickering.

4

Halfway down his body, he jiggled, but of course I didn't look.

Instead, I bent over halfway, sticking my rear out in his direction. "You really think so?" I said, squirming back and forth.

"Middlebrook!" Kevin said, all teeth and whiskers and dimples. "You are such a fag!"

Mission accomplished, I thought. My cover was holding—for another day at least.

Once I'd finished dressing, I met up with my friends Gunnar and Min for lunch at our usual table in the school cafeteria.

"The paint is flaking off the ceiling in Mr. Wick's classroom," Gunnar said as we started to eat. "Sometimes the chips land on my desk." Gunnar and I had been friends forever, or at least since the fourth grade, when his family had moved from Norway to my neighborhood. I'd always thought he should be proud of being from somewhere different, but kids had teased him about his accent and his name (they called him "Goony" or "Gunner"), so he desperately tried to ignore his heritage. Gunnar was a thoroughly nice guy and perfectly loyal as a friend, but—and this is hard to admit, him being a buddy and all—just a little bit high-strung.

"It's an old school," Min said. "The whole ceiling's going to collapse on us one of these days." Min was the school egghead. (She was also Chinese American, which is something of a stereotype, isn't it?) But unlike Shelly Vorhaus, the school's other egghead, Min had more than two shirts and actually wore makeup. In other words, Min and Gunnar were both like me, occasional visitors to the border region of high school respectability.

"You don't understand," Gunnar said to Min. "What if it's lead paint? You said it yourself: this is an old building."

"Lead paint?" I said.

"You know—the kind that causes brain damage if you ingest it?" Gunnar could also be a bit of a hypochondriac or whatever.

"So what if it is?" Min said. "You're not eating it, are you?"

"Ingest doesn't just mean to eat something," Gunnar said. "It can also mean to inhale. Most people don't know that." He was right; I hadn't known that. But if Min didn't know it either, I didn't feel so bad.

I liked Min and Gunnar. We had a lot in common, and for the most part, I felt comfortable around them. But I couldn't help wondering how they'd react if they knew my little secret—my liking guys, I mean. I doubted they'd run shrieking from the room. But they were my best friends, and I couldn't have handled anything less than confetti-and-sparklers acceptance. Which was why I'd decided never to tell them. But which was also why I guess I never felt *that* comfortable around them.

Suddenly, a blanket of silence fell across the cafeteria. Min, Gunnar, and I all turned to see what was making the lack of a commotion.

Brian Bund, a junior, was sitting by himself at a table in the corner, his hunched, bony back to the room. Someone had flung a big spoonful of chili at him, and it had spattered across the back of his white T-shirt.

As soon as people realized what had happened, they began to laugh. I glanced around the lunchroom. Ordinarily, there was a cafeteria worker or two around, cleaning tables or refilling napkin dispensers, but there were no adults just then—which was probably why Brian had been on the receiving end of the chili in the first place.

A lot of people were laughing at Brian now, but the jocks, sitting two tables away from him, were laughing the loudest. I was certain the projectile chili was their handiwork. Sure enough, even as the whole lunchroom was watching, Jarred Gasner lobbed a spoonful of chocolate pudding at the back of Brian's shirt. And Nate Klane flicked a heap of vanilla ice cream at him. Kevin Land, snickering with the rest of the jocks, wasn't throwing anything, but he'd probably been the one to throw the chili that had started it all. But at least I had to give those jocks credit for their aim, because everything they threw hit Brian square in the hair or back.

By now, the cafeteria was ringing with laughter. It was coming from every corner of the room. The cheerleaders at the Cheerleaders table. The druggies at the Druggies table. And the Girl Jocks, the Theater Crowd, and the Lefty Radicals at all their tables too. Even some of the kids at the Christians, Orchestra Members, and Computer Geeks tables were laughing. (For the record, Min, Gunnar, and I made up the Nerdy Intellectuals, and no one at our table was laughing.)

I wasn't surprised by any of this. Brian Bund was the unquestioned outcast of the school. The jocks teased him mercilessly, and almost everyone else watched and laughed while they did it. Maybe Brian would be one of those high school outcasts you read about who grow up, found some software company, and make fifty billion dollars. But for the time being, he was the lowest of the low, and all the future billions that he might someday make wouldn't get me to trade places with him.

I'd like to be able to say that when I saw what was being done to him, I stood up and spoke out, stopping the humiliation with some cheeky quip. If this had been the movie of my life, that's exactly what I would have done—a great way to establish what a plucky, likeable guy I am. But this wasn't a movie, and the only audience was the other kids in that cafeteria, so I sat there like everyone else. It wouldn't have made any difference anyway. Nothing I could've said would have stopped what they were doing to Brian. The jocks just would've thrown stuff at me too, and when I took life-saving, the first thing they taught us was to think long and hard before you approach a drowning person— that if you get too close, they can pull you under with them.

*"What's going on?"* The voice of a cafeteria worker cut through the din.

The food stopped coming, but the laughter didn't.

Brian sat there for a second, the back of his shirt flecked with chili and ice cream and pudding. Then he stood up, and bits of food started dripping down to the floor. Brian turned and looked out across the cafeteria with such a mixture of bewilderment and sadness in his eyes that I felt a deep pang of a shame way down in my stomach, even though I was one of only about fifteen people who weren't laughing at him. Incredibly, Brian took the time to carry his tray to the garbage can, where he dumped his trash. Anyone who couldn't see the dignity in his sorting of his dirty silverware didn't know what dignity was.

But most of the kids in the cafeteria just laughed louder still.

"Would you *look* at this?" said the frustrated cafeteria worker, spotting the mess behind where Brian had been sitting. "Who's going to clean this up? Huh? *Who?*" The worker was saying this to Brian, which I thought was ironic. Talk about blaming the victim.

Gunnar, Min, and I turned back to our table, but none of us said anything. I wasn't sure what Gunnar and Min were thinking. I knew they thought it was terrible how everyone treated Brian Bund. But let's face it, Brian was weird. He had acne and he smelled bad. And to Gunnar and Min, Brian probably seemed so different that he was like another species. You care when someone kicks a dog, you feel bad for the poor animal, but you don't feel that bad, because it's not like it's a human being.

Brian didn't seem so different to me. Because I knew that's how people might treat me if they ever learned the truth. It scared the hell out of me, because I was certain I could never handle being that completely alone.

That night in my bedroom, I logged on to the Net. I said I'd never actually been naked with a guy, but it's possible that once or twice I might've gone to a gay chat room and maybe even gone off for a private chat with a guy or two. I refuse to say any more about this on the grounds that it may incriminate me, but I will say that mostly we really did just chat about innocent things, like how long had we known we were gay and which actor did we think was cute.

The fact is, there's a difference between being alone and being lonely; I may not have been completely alone in life, but I was definitely lonely. My secret mission—four years in an American high school—had been an involuntary one, and now I desperately wanted to be somewhere where I could be honest about who I was and what I wanted. I had plenty to say on the topic, but no one to say it to—not my friends, definitely not my parents (don't get me started). The Internet gave me people to say it to. Problem is, they weren't real.

That night, I visited one of my regular gay haunts. Among the list of various chat rooms—"College Students," "Bisexuals," "Political Junkies," etc.— there is a whole list of rooms categorized by geographic location. In other words, if you want to talk to a gay person in Boise, Idaho, there's a room labeled "Boise, Idaho."

I kept scrolling down the screen until I came to a room listing the town where I live. It hadn't been here before—they must have just added it—and it caught me by surprise. My hometown is kind of smallish, and it had never occurred to me that there might actually be other gay people there. It made sense, of course— 10 percent, gays are your friends and neighbors, all that crap. But I'd kind of assumed that that's just talk and that gay people really only live in New York and San Francisco. Still, if there are gay people in Boise, Idaho, it stood to reason they'd be in my town too.

I entered the chat room. I may have been a tad more excited than usual.

There was only one other person in the room, which made sense to me, since I figured there was only about one other gay person in my whole hometown. His handle was GayTeen, which wasn't the most original name I'd ever seen. Mine was Smuggler, for no reason I can explain.

*Hey,* I wrote.

*'Sup?* he wrote.

Not exactly the most exciting conversation. But I admit, I was desperate.

*Age?* I asked.

*16,* he wrote back. Of course, I had no way of knowing that anything he said was true—the good or bad part of the Internet, depending on what you looked like. On the other hand, if it was some creepy old guy looking to bust a nut, it would become clear pretty quickly, and I could just check myself out.

I asked him if he really lived in my town.

*Sure,* he wrote.

*Where u go to school?* I asked. This was a test. There are three high schools in the area—it isn't *that* small a town—but if he really lived nearby, he'd know the schools.

The screen was empty for a second, like GayTeen was thinking. Then a word appeared. *Goodkind.*

I hadn't expected this. This was *my* high school! I could accept that there were other gay people in my town, even other high school students. But I definitely could *not* accept that they went to my high school! Once again, I knew it made sense. But I'd just felt so lonely for so long, it had never occurred to me that I might not have to feel that way.

Was it someone I knew?

*What year are u?* I asked.

*Sophomore,* he wrote back. *U?*

*Same,* I wrote. Well, that clinched it. I knew everyone in my class, at least by name. Whoever this was, I had to know him.

We chatted for a few more minutes, mostly about teachers and cafeteria food. There was no denying that he was a student and he went to my school. He knew too much not to.

Finally, my curiosity got the best of me. *Who are u?* I wrote. *What's your real name?* I had to know.

The screen stayed blank. GayTeen didn't answer.

*Are u still there?* I wrote.

*I'm here,* GayTeen wrote. *Who are u? You tell me first.*

Suddenly, I saw the problem. If I told GayTeen who I was, there was no guarantee he'd tell me who he was. And if he didn't, he could tell people about me. If he told me who he was and I didn't respond, I could do the same thing to him. We could promise to write our names at exactly the same time, but who's to say we'd both do it?

No. We couldn't reveal ourselves over the Internet. The stakes were far too high.

Two new words appeared on my screen. *Let's meet,* they said.

I knew immediately that this was the logical solution. It was the only way to even out the risk. We'd see each other at the same time. He'd know about me, but I'd know about him too. If he talked about me, I could talk about him—mutually assured destruction.

The risk was lower, true, but there was still a risk. I'd never actually met a known gay person before. Did it really make sense for the first one to be someone from my class? After the lengths I'd gone to over the years to conceal my true identity, how could I even consider entrusting that information to someone I didn't know? I'd never even told Min or Gunnar.

All this flashed through my mind, but even as it did, I was typing a response so fast my fingers were stumbling over the keys. It was only a single word: *Where?*

It was well past dark when I arrived at the play field where we'd agreed to meet. I locked my bike and scanned the area, but I didn't see anyone. There weren't any cars in the parking lot either. The air was cool and wet, and I was shivering even under a heavy jacket, but it wasn't just from the cold.

Then I saw him. There's a picnic gazebo on the far side of the field, which borders a dense swampy area. Under the gazebo, a dark figure sat hunched atop a picnic table. Even as I spotted him, he seemed to see me too. He slipped off the table, stepping forward, still in the shadows, but peering out into the darkness.

The moon was behind some soggy clouds, so I couldn't see him clearly, and he couldn't see me. In other words, I could still back out. I could unlock my bike, climb aboard, and pedal away, and he'd never know who I was. But I knew I wasn't going to. I'd already come too far.

I started across the field. It had been raining a lot lately, and the grass had flooded. The mud sucked at my tennis shoes, cold water seeping into my socks.

Who was it under that picnic gazebo? I could tell from his slightly slackened posture that it really was a high school student—but who? What if it was Gunnar? No, it was probably Brian Bund. What would I do then? I couldn't very well just turn my back on him and leave.

I passed a children's play area to one side of the

field—two sets of rusted metal monkey bars, one in the shape of a covered wagon, the other in the shape of a tepee, in the middle of a patch of flooded sand.

The figure in the gazebo hadn't made any movement toward me, but he hadn't backed away either. He just stood there watching me. The only thing more fitting would have been if he'd been smoking a cigarette and wearing a dark overcoat.

This was stupid. I'd talked to dozens of gay teenagers on the Internet. I'd told *them* I was gay. What was the difference? But even as I thought this, I knew the difference, and it was big. This was real.

I was less than thirty feet from the gazebo now. The methane stench from the swamp was foul, and I couldn't imagine anyone ever actually having a picnic here. A few more feet, and we'd be able to see each other clearly. I was risking everything, but for what I wasn't sure. All I knew was that I'd been undercover for far too long. It was time to finally make contact.

Taking a deep breath, I sloshed the rest of the way across the grass, stepped into the gazebo, and found myself staring into the dark, bristled face of Kevin Land.

## CHAPTER TWO

I'd made a mistake. I must have come to the wrong picnic gazebo in the wrong park, probably even on the wrong night.

"Kevin?" I said. "What are you doing here?"

Kevin, meanwhile, looked just as surprised to see me. "Russel?" he said, then quickly added, "Nothing! What are *you* doing here?" There was no mistaking it—Kevin was nervous.

"I was out for a ride on my bike," I said, glancing around. Now *I* was nervous. I knew I didn't really have the wrong gazebo or the wrong time. GayTeen just hadn't shown up yet. But what if he showed up now? If he went to Goodkind High School and he was in my class, he'd know Kevin Land. He might say something to him about me.

"Yeah?" Kevin said, way too loud. "Well, I was just out for a walk!" Without another word, he started walking away then and there.

That's when I finally realized that—duh!—Kevin was the one I'd come here to see. It had just never occurred to me that Kevin Land—*Kevin Land!*—could be gay, not even after finding him in the exact spot where I'd arranged to meet a gay teenager from my school.

"GayTeen," I said to Kevin. It wasn't a question.

He stopped in his tracks, his back to me. But he didn't say anything. He looked like he wasn't even breathing.

Finally, he whirled on me, anger in his eyes. "What the hell does that mean? Are you calling me a fag or what?"

If this had been the Kevin Land I knew from the school, the swaggering, confident guy in the locker room after gym class, I might have fallen for this. But it wasn't. This was an entirely different Kevin Land, one with hunched shoulders and a catch in his voice. And unlike the other Kevin Land, this one had not only anger in his eyes, but also fear.

"Kevin," I said. "Knock it off. I know you're GayTeen."

Kevin's eyes went wider still, and it seemed like I could read his thoughts. Should I deny it? he was thinking. And, should I try to intimidate him?

"Relax," I said, oddly serene. "I'm not going to tell anyone." I'd been afraid of how risky it was, meeting like this, but now I saw that I held the power here. It was true—Kevin could start a rumor about me, tell everyone at school that I was gay. But I could start a rumor about him too, and let's face it, I was just Russel Middlebrook. He, on the other hand, was Kevin Land, Baseball Jock Incorporated. He had a hell of a lot more to lose.

Finally, Kevin sighed, as if in defeat. His whole body seemed to crumple. He drifted closer to me again but wouldn't look me in the eye.

"So Kevin Land is gay," I said. I tried, but I couldn't wipe the smirk off my face. After years of teasing by Kevin and guys just like him, it was fun to have the upper hand for a change.

"Shhh!" Kevin said, and it echoed across the grass. "Besides, I don't know what I am."

"You look at pictures of naked guys on the Internet?"

He hesitated. "Sometimes."

"You're gay. What's the big deal?" I was enjoying this way too much, but I still couldn't stop myself.

"The big deal," Kevin said, "is that nobody at Goodkind knows about me! And they *can't* know! If they knew I screwed around with guys—!"

"You've had sex with guys?" I hadn't expected this. Gay, yes—sexually active, no.

"Maybe," Kevin said. He glanced over, met my gaze at last, but now I looked away. The next logical question was for him to ask me if I'd had sex with a guy, which I hadn't, but I sure as hell didn't want to tell him that, so I was suddenly desperate to change the subject.

"Who would ever have a picnic here?" I said, now talking too loudly myself. "I mean, it stinks! Don't you think that swamp sure stinks?"

Kevin saw right through me. "Never had sex, huh?" Suddenly, he was the old Kevin Land again, the one with the smirk and the upper hand.

"Well," I said, "not with a guy." Notice the careful wording on this. I wasn't actually saying I'd had sex with a girl, because I hadn't. But it was phrased in such a way to make Kevin think that I had. Clever, huh?

"It doesn't matter," Kevin said, his smirk fading as

quickly as it had appeared. I had to give him credit. He could have made me squirm like I had him, but he hadn't.

"So now we know about each other," I said. "Now what?" I had a few ideas, but I wasn't going to be the one to suggest them.

"I don't know," Kevin said. "I guess we could talk."

"Okay. Let's talk."

And what do you know? That's exactly what we did.


The next day at school, Kevin Land didn't ignore me. If I was reading this, that's what I would think would've happened, but it's not what did happen. Kevin acknowledged me in the hall, talked to me in gym class. He wasn't super-chummy, but if he had been all friendly, people would have noticed, and that was something neither of us wanted. Pacing around that cold, stinky gazebo the night before, Kevin and I had talked for over an hour. He'd told me how out of place he felt around his jock friends, and that all his macho posturing in the locker room was really just an act to make sure no one ever questioned his sexuality or whatever. At first, this had sounded a little like Santa

Claus saying he was allergic to reindeer, but Kevin had seemed sincere, so I gave him the benefit of the doubt. I had told Kevin that I felt out of place too, but I'd left out the part about feeling lonely, because I thought it sounded a little too Oprah. We'd agreed to get together again soon to talk some more. After our first day back at school, I now thought we might actually do it.

For the first time in my life, I was friends with (a) one of the most popular kids in school, and (b) an actual gay person. Incredibly, they were the same person. This had to be one of those ironic plot twists my English teacher was always blathering on about.

That night after school, I met my friend Gunnar by the bike rack. Since we lived on the same block, we usually rode home together, talking all the way. But that day, my head was spinning. I was thinking about Kevin, about all we'd talked about the night before, and maybe a little bit about what he looked like naked in the locker room.

Of course, I couldn't mention any of this to Gunnar. Besides, he had other things on his mind.

"I think Mr. Kluger is purposely making the fluorescent lights in his psychology classroom flicker in order to keep us drowsy," Gunnar said.

Before long, we reached the base of a long, low hill that had to be climbed to get home. Coming to school in the mornings, I loved this hill, because I was going downhill and because I was usually running late. But in the afternoons, man, did I hate this hill.

"I wish I had a girlfriend," Gunnar said out of the blue, just as we'd started pedaling for the top. This didn't surprise me. Gunnar had wanted a girlfriend for as long as I'd known him. "A girlfriend or a dog," he added.

"A dog?" I said, confused. "What does a dog have to do with a girlfriend?" Gunnar's brain was like a giant ball of string; in the end, everything tied together, but it was impossible to see exactly how. This was actually one of things I liked most about him.

Gunnar sighed. "Every popular guy I've ever known has had a girlfriend or a dog. Sometimes both. But the best I can hope for is a girlfriend who *is* a dog."

"You don't want a dog," I said. "They spend half their time licking their butts, and they still stink."

"Fine, forget the dog. But I *do* want a girlfriend!" Gunnar was out of breath, and only partly from the uphill ride.

"Because it means you're not a loser."

"Exactly! And don't deny it, because you know it's true."

"Kinda crass," I said. "What if the girl finds out you're only dating her to be more popular?"

"Are you kidding? Girls already know it. It's even worse for them. After all, they don't have the dog to fall back on."

Even when I was almost positive Gunnar was making a joke, I couldn't be certain he was. But I knew he wasn't joking about the added status he thought a girlfriend would give him. And to be absolutely frank, Gunnar was right about the whole girlfriend/status connection. He was also right that status was something he could have used a little more of. Gunnar was no Brian Bund, but he was definitely an acquired taste.

"So," Gunnar said as we reached the crest of the hill. "Will you help?"

"Help what?" I said. Now we were both gasping for air.

"Help me get a girlfriend!"

"Why me?"

"I don't know. You seem more relaxed around girls." This was true. It was the naked Kevin Lands of the world who tied my stomach into knots. Why the whole world hadn't long since concluded I was gay, I honestly didn't know.

"What about Min?" I said.

"What about her?"

"I mean as a girlfriend."

"Too cerebral." I didn't point out the obvious—that anyone who used words like "cerebral" sounded to me like a perfect match for Min.

We started down the hill. I'd always loved the coast down the opposite side of an uphill climb, with the wind blowing in my face.

"So you'll help me?" Gunnar called.

"Help you what?"

"Get a girlfriend!"

"Sure," I said. "Whatever I can do." This was an easy promise to make. Gunnar had been trying to get a girlfriend forever, and he'd never even come close.

I was dying to tell someone about Kevin Land. This makes me sound like a jerk, I know, but what can I say? The heart wants what it wants, and my heart wanted to dish dirt on Kevin Land. I had no desire to spread it all over school. I just wanted to tell one single person—to say the news out loud, so I'd know I wasn't imagining things. The problem was, in order to tell anyone about Kevin, I first had to tell them about me. That meant it had to be someone I could trust. Gunnar was out—I had no idea how he'd react to the information. That left Min. I know I said before how I'd decided to never tell her about myself, but meeting Kevin Land had somehow changed my mind.

That Saturday afternoon, Min and I were over at her house playing a game of Wiz War in her bedroom. We were keeping score on the folded front page of the *Goodkind Gazette*, the school newspaper; I was surprised that Min even had a copy, since no one ever read the *Goodkind Gazette*. I was winning the game but was taking nothing for granted. Wiz War is the kind of game where you think the outcome is absolutely inevitable—and then the other player draws a single card that changes everything.

"So," I said, pretending to stare at my cards, but really thinking about what I was going to tell her. "How do you feel about malicious gossip?"

"Hmm?" Min said, barely listening, glaring at the game board like she could change it through the sheer force of her will.

"Gossip," I said. "I learned something interesting about someone at our school."

She placed down a card. "I hit you with a fireball."

I stared at the pieces on the board. "You can't cast a fireball. There's no line of sight."

A smile slid across her face, and she laid down a

second card. "Vision-stone," she said. "I can see through walls."

I countered her fireball with a card of my own, but her vision-stone card was reusable, which was not a good development for me.

"So," Min said. "What's this gossip?" Now that the tide was turning in her favor, her mood had brightened considerably. Min didn't like to lose. Fortunately for her, she rarely did.

"Oh," I said. "That." I stared at my cards for real now, then played a spell of my own—a stun card—which Min immediately countered.

"Come on," she said. "Spill the beans."

"It's about Kevin Land."

"What about him?" She laid down a waterbolt card, which I also countered.

"What would you say if I told you Kevin Land was gay?"

Min arched an eyebrow. "I'd say that *is* interesting. How do you know?"

The moment of truth. Rather than meet her gaze, I concentrated on the game board, moving my wizard as far away from hers as I could.

"I ran into him in a gay chat room," I said softly. "We didn't know who the other was until we agreed to meet. I don't know who was more surprised, him or me."

Min stared at me, absolutely frozen. Even her pupils didn't move.

I looked down at the board again. "I know what you're thinking," I said, fumbling with the points on the triangular die. "You're thinking, What was I doing in a gay chat room?"

Min didn't say anything, but she wasn't stupid. She knew exactly what I'd just told her.

I put down a thought-steal card—one of the few attack cards that didn't require line of sight. "Counter that," I said.

Min began to laugh.

"What?" I said. "What's so funny?"

But she just laughed even louder. Before long, she looked like she was going to pop a blood vessel in her neck.

"Min," I said. "It's not that funny." This wasn't the reaction I'd expected at all. To tell the truth, she was kind of pissing me off.

"It's not you," Min said, winding down, wiping away a tear. "I'm not laughing at you."

"Then what?"

"You know Terese Buckman?"

"The soccer player?" I said. She went to our school, but I barely knew her.

Min nodded. "What would you say if I told you she was a lesbian?"

"Really? Wow." I can't say I was wildly surprised. She was kind of butch. Still, that meant there were three gay students at my high school—exactly two more than I would've guessed.

Min took a deep breath, held it, then let it go. "And what would you say if I told you she was my girlfriend?"

"I know she's your girlfriend. Weren't you in the Girl Scouts together?"

"No," Min said, suddenly dead serious. "I mean my *girlfriend*."

This time, it was me who froze.

Now Min wouldn't look me in the eye. Instead, she played a series of cards, first countering my last attack, then knocking down walls and opening doors, until there was only a single wall between me and her. Then she laid down one final card, the sudden death spell. Since she'd already forced me to use up my last counteraction card, she had me. She won. I was dead.

At last, she peeked up at me. "Well?"

"You're gay?"

"Actually, I think bisexual is probably more accurate." Never in a million years would I have guessed that Min was bisexual. And yet, now that she'd told me, it already made perfect sense. In a way, it explained everything from her general braininess to her ridiculous perfectionism.

I started laughing. Suddenly, I couldn't stop myself! Almost at once, Min joined in. Soon we were both rolling around on the floor of her room, cackling like barnyard animals.

Okay, this was too weird. Was the whole school secretly gay or what?

## CHAPTER THREE

The next night, I IMed Kevin and asked him to meet me at the stinky picnic gazebo.

"'Sup?" he said when I got there. Was it my imagination, or did he actually look happy to see me?

"Not much," I said.

Then Kevin's expression changed from being happy to see me to looking like he expected me to say something else—like he expected me to have a reason for our little get-together. But I didn't have a reason. I'd just wanted to talk some more.

"I just found out my friend, Min, has a girlfriend," I said. "Terese Buckman?" I hadn't planned on telling him this, but I couldn't really think of anything else to say, and besides, Min had said it was okay.

"Min's a big ol' lesbo, huh?" Kevin said. Kevin was gay, but he could still sound like kind of a stupid jock sometimes. I wish I could say I was shocked and appalled by this, but I actually thought it was kind of cute (okay, really cute).

"I think the word she used was 'bisexual,'" I said.

"And Buckman's a dyke too? Can't say that one comes as a total shock."

I never knew what to say when someone said stuff like this. It was one thing to think it. It was another thing to say it out loud.

"You have any gay friends?" I asked.

Kevin shook his head. "Nope. Not that I know of."

We both got quiet. I'd hoped we could talk about Min and Terese at least a little longer, but the conversation hadn't really gone anywhere. So we just kind of stood there with our hands in our pockets, staring out at the grass.

"Well . . . ," Kevin said, like he was thinking about leaving.

"We should meet!" I blurted.

"Huh?" Kevin said. "Who?"

"Min and Terese and you and me! That's what I

wanted to tell you. We could all get together after school. We could get a pizza or something." This was a lie. I hadn't wanted to tell Kevin this, and I didn't particularly want to get together with Min and Terese. But I'd been desperate for something—anything!—to say. But now that I'd said it, it didn't seem like such a horrible idea. If nothing else, it'd give me a chance to spend more time with Kevin. I just hoped he wouldn't embarrass me by calling them lesbos and dykes.

"Oh," Kevin said. He pondered for a second, looking like he was calculating the odds on a poker hand. But finally, he looked up at me and said, "Okay. I mean, why not? I've never known any lesbians before."

All of us wanted something different on our pizza. It was after school on Wednesday, and Kevin, Min, Terese, and I had come to a pizza place not far from school. Now that I knew for a fact that Terese was a LESBIAN (in capital letters), she didn't look so much like one anymore. Sure, she had cropped blond hair and, frankly, broader shoulders than me. But she also had these great cheekbones and these really pretty baby blue eyes. She almost could've modeled or something.

Terese had brought a friend, Ike, who she'd whispered was "one of us," which I knew meant he was gay. Ike was a tall, lanky, sort of nervous guy with a wispy goatee and a bandanna over his head. I'd seen him around school, but I'd never actually talked to him. He hung with the lefty activist crowd—they'd had this bust of a rally for animal rights a couple of months ago.

But here we were in this little hole-in-the-wall pizza place with no windows, and booths made of orange vinyl, and we couldn't agree on a pizza. Kevin and Terese both wanted meat, but Kevin wanted ground beef and sausage, and Terese wanted Canadian bacon. Min and Ike were vegetarians, but Ike didn't like mushrooms and Min hated olives. As for me, I wanted anchovies and artichoke hearts, but I knew enough not to even bother suggesting this to a group of teenagers.

We finally got it together and ordered one pepperoni and one vegetarian with no mushrooms or olives. Then we took the booth farthest in the back, like we were spies having a rendezvous to talk about something top secret, which I guess we kind of were.

For the first few minutes, we sat around making chitchat with the people each of us knew. That meant I talked mostly to Min or Kevin, and Terese talked mostly to Min or Ike. It felt like right before the start of a class, when you sit there and gab with your friends. But it also felt different from right before class, because there was this definite undercurrent of excitement in the air, like we were waiting for something interesting or important to happen.

They brought us our pizzas, and we all stared down at them in silence. I suddenly felt this sense of disappointment from everyone, like we all realized at the same time that the pizzas were the only thing we'd been waiting for—that nothing else interesting or important was going to happen after all.

We started chowing down, and still nobody said anything, except stuff like, "It's good," or "Can I get a napkin?" It was strange. Now that the pizzas had arrived, it was like we couldn't talk in groups of two or three anymore. For some reason, now we all had to talk together as a group.

Things stayed quiet. Ike scratched a tattoo. Finally I said, "So. Here we are." I sounded like an idiot, I know, but it just seemed like I had to say something. After all, this little get-together had been my idea.

"Yeah," Min said. "Here we are." She obviously felt some responsibility too, maybe because she'd suggested this gathering to Terese, who'd even brought Ike.

No one said anything, and I was particularly annoyed with Kevin, just sitting there gulping down pizza like a homeless man at a soup kitchen. He was supposed to be my friend. Couldn't he at least *try* to help keep this meal from dying an agonizing death?

He kicked back in his seat and looked over at Terese. "You guys got a good team this year?"

Okay, I thought, maybe he isn't so thick after all.

"'Sokay," Terese said. "We lost a couple of seniors last year, but most of our talent is sophomores anyway. Our goalie's a freshman."

"Wish we could say that," Kevin said. "We lost our pitcher and most of our hitters. We're goin' begging."

Terese looked like she was going to say something else, but then she seemed to realize that no one else was talking. And like I said before, suddenly it seemed like whatever was said was being said to the whole group. So she fell silent.

I thought, So much for sports as a topic of conversation.

Ike stared down at the pizza. "You know they genetically modify tomatoes?" he said. "They tried to make them redder, and it worked, but they ended up really small. And now they've made tomatoes that can grow in salt water."

"Oh!" Min said, perking up. "Is that like when they took genes from a flounder and inserted them into strawberry plants, so the berries wouldn't be killed by frost?"

Ike nodded excitedly. "I heard they somehow crossed a goat with a spider."

"There's a joke in there somewhere," I quipped. "Something about Little Miss Muffet eating the spider's curds and whey." I was trying to be funny, but no one laughed except Min, who only chuckled. Ike didn't even smile, and I decided I didn't like him very much. Then I saw him glance over at Kevin, and his gaze seemed to linger. I thought, Why is he looking at Kevin? Min and I were the ones who'd been talking. That's when I knew the real reason I didn't like Ike: he wanted to move in on Kevin.

"Know what else they do?" Ike was saying. "Seed companies change plants' genes so they can't make any new seeds. Then they sell the seeds really cheap, like in third world countries. That way, farmers have to keep buying new seeds again year after year. And once the farmers are hooked, the companies slowly raise the prices."

This time, it was Min who looked like she was going to say something. But like Terese a few minutes earlier, she seemed to sense that most of us weren't interested in this topic either, so she didn't speak up.

So much for politics.

Here we were, halfway through our pizzas, and it was suddenly clear that, as a group, we had nothing in common whatsoever. We were just five random people. Why should we hit it off just because we all happened to be gay? It was stupid. Ridiculous.

"We're all alone," I said.

It was quiet for a second. Then Terese said, "Man, is that true."

"Sure can't tell your family," Kevin said. "My dad would go feral."

"Mine too," Min said. "I'm not even sure my mom knows what 'gay' is. And even if I could get her to understand that, how do I ever get her to understand 'bisexual'?"

"Can't tell your friends either," Ike said, staring down at the pizza again, but not at the tomatoes this time. "Even if they say they're radical. They're not radical about this. Not when they're still in high school."

Of course, what I'd meant when I'd said "We're all alone" was that there were no other customers in the pizza joint. I'd just been trying to make conversation. I hadn't been talking about being gay at all. But it had finally got the conversation rolling, so I wasn't about to explain what I'd really meant.

"It's not like I don't have friends," Terese was saying, playing with her crusts. "I got a lot of friends. Sometimes they rank on me about being a dyke or a homo, but they don't believe it, not really. I know what they'd say if they knew they were right. So it's like you can never really relax, not when you're with other people. I mean, if they knew the truth, would they still be your friends?"

*Yes!* I thought. That was exactly how I felt! During our talk at the stinky picnic gazebo, Kevin had said he felt this way too. Did that mean all gay kids felt like this?

"It's like you're always wearing a mask or whatever," Ike said. "Your family, even your friends, you can't let them see the real you."

I hated to admit it, what with Ike saying it and all, but this described how I felt too.

"It's hard," Kevin said. "Damn, it's hard."

It was strange hearing Kevin sound so serious. I was curious to know exactly what he meant, so I asked, "What is?"

He shrugged, his eyes downcast. "You know. Stuff. I guess that's why I used to drink so much. Not just with my friends. Sometimes even when I was alone. I mean, it's hard keeping a secret like this. Can't talk about what you're really feeling. Especially when you're a jock or whatever. You probably think it's great being popular, and yeah, sometimes it is. But there's pressure. Sometimes, there's so much pressure, it feels like you're gonna burst! You wanna be honest and open, even if it's just with yourself. But it's hard. Sometimes, it's just so damn hard."

"I know," Min said. "If it wasn't for Terese these past three years, I don't know what I would've done." Min glanced around the pizza place, which was still empty. Then she took Terese's hand. "Probably gone insane," Min said.

"I tried to kill myself," Ike said. (If you ever want to stop a conversation dead in its tracks, say these five words with a really serious expression on your face.)

We all looked at him.

"Don't worry," Ike said with a half smile. "It was a long time ago. I was fourteen. It was so stupid. Someone told me you could kill yourself if you drank dishwashing liquid. It just made me really really sick. I had to go to the hospital and everything. But when I drank it, I really wanted to die. I told everyone it was because my Science Fair project hadn't won a ribbon, and my parents actually believed me. But the truth was, I was just tired of trying so hard to not be gay." He looked around the table. "I never told anyone that before. I never even told my therapist."

When Ike said all this, I felt bad for before, when I'd thought I didn't like him.

"Well, someone say something else!" Ike said, already flushing red. "Otherwise, it'll seem like I killed the conversation."

We all laughed. Then, just to get things started again, I told everyone how I'd been so lonely I'd been willing to meet some kid I didn't know—some kid I'd met one night on a computer—at a park in the middle of the night. Kevin smiled when I said this.

We kept talking, and I thought, Except for Min, I don't know these people—I don't really even know Kevin. But it was like I could be completely honest for the first time in my life. We were telling each other things we'd never told our best friends before, things we'd never even said out loud.

The five of us may have been alone in the pizza place, but we weren't really alone. Not anymore.

After we'd been talking for a while, the door to the pizza parlor burst open, and a couple of husky construction workers sauntered inside.

They were a good thirty feet away from our table—they were up at the counter trying to decide on a pizza—but we all stopped talking anyway.

Finally, Terese looked down at her watch and said, "Damn! It's after six." We'd been there for three hours. It had seemed like about five minutes.

No one moved. We all just stared down at the wadded napkins on the empty pizza pans. I think we all knew it was time to head home, but no one wanted to let the moment end.

"I wish we could stay," Min said.

"Yeah," Kevin said.

"This so sucks," Terese said.

There was another pause. Then Ike said, "It doesn't have to. Suck, I mean."

We all looked at him.

"I mean, why couldn't we meet again tomorrow? At school? We could eat lunch together."

It took a second for the idea to sink in.

"Why not?" I said.

"Sounds good!" Min said.

"I'm in!" Terese said.

Once we'd decided this, it made it a hell of a lot easier to leave. After all, it's not like the conversation was over. We were just suspending it for a while.

We all walked out to our cars and bikes, and then spent another forty minutes or so standing around talking some more. However much we said to each other, there always seemed to be more to say. And no matter what anyone said, it seemed like everyone else understood it perfectly. I couldn't help but wonder if this was always the way it felt around good friends when you don't have to hide who you are.

That's when I remembered the beginning of the meal, and how it had seemed like we were all waiting for some really interesting and important thing to happen. Now I knew that it had happened after all.

## CHAPTER FOUR

"You like him," Min said to me a few minutes later, after we'd thrown my bike into the back of her parents' Honda, and she was driving me home.

"What?" I said uneasily. "Who?"

"Russel, please," Min said. "Kevin. You like Kevin."

"I do not!" I was shocked and appalled by the suggestion. I was also stunned that Min had picked up on it so quickly. What had given me away?

"No?" Min said.

"No!" I said.

"Well, you have to admit he's hot."

"No, I don't!"

Min looked over at me from the driver's seat. "Oh, Russel, come on. He *is* hot. Bisexual, remember?"

Something told me that wouldn't be the first time I'd hear those words.

"So?" she said.

"So what?" I said.

"So don't you think he's hot?"

"I already told you. No."

Min slowly shook her head. "That is so sad. You can't even admit when a guy's hot. And when we were all being so honest back there at the pizza place."

"Okay!" I said.

"Okay, what?"

"What you said."

Min smiled. "So say it."

"Say what?"

"Say you think Kevin Land is hot."

"Min!"

"What's the big deal? Why can't you say it?"

"Okay, I think Kevin Land is hot! Happy?"

She slapped the dashboard in victory. "*Ha!* I knew it! I *knew* you liked him!"

Like I said, Min liked to win. This was another example of that. But she hadn't won yet. I could still change the subject.

*"Three years?"* I said. "You've been with Terese for *three years*, and you never bothered to tell me?"

Now it was Min's turn to blush. "It wasn't like that," she said. "We met at Girl Scout camp. At first, it was just this weird inseparable/infatuation thing, except I didn't know it was infatuation. The sex didn't come until later on." Sex, I thought. There was that word again.

"But she had her friends, and I had mine," Min went on. "They didn't really mix. So we never told anyone. Not just that we're together. Not even that we're friends. We meet in this old warehouse down on Fracton. All these years, my parents think I've been doing volunteer work down at the YMCA. Twisted is what it is. Really sick and neurotic and twisted." She looked over at me again and scrunched up her face in embarrassment. "And I *love* it!"

I laughed, then stared out at the darkening road in front of us. The days were getting longer, but they weren't very long yet.

"I guess I do like Kevin," I said at last. It was a relief to finally say it out loud. But kind of scary too.

Min just smiled. She liked to win, but at least she didn't rub it in when she did.

"But it's stupid," I said. "Kevin Land? I mean,

what's the point?" I wasn't fishing for compliments. This is really what I thought. In an infinite number of possible universes, I couldn't imagine even one universe where Kevin and I got together.

That's why I almost fell out of the car when Min just smiled again and said, very casually, "Yeah, I think he likes you too."

The next morning, on my way to third period P.E., I happened to walk by the office of Mr. Rall, the school principal. The door was open, and I heard heated voices coming from inside.

"I will *not* be censored in my own classroom!" said a voice. It was Ms. Toles, the health teacher, and she had that little quiver of indignation in her voice that people get when they're absolutely convinced they're right, and they can't believe that anyone would even suggest otherwise.

"Corrine, please," Mr. Rall said. "Let's all try to stay calm."

"I'm sorry, David, but what you're saying is just not acceptable!"

"Not *acceptable*?" came a second male voice, with exactly the same quiver of indignation that Ms. Toles had. "I'll tell you what's not acceptable! Making obscene gestures to a classroom full of teenagers!"

I skidded to a stop in the hallway. Adults arguing about sex? Suddenly, this was getting good. And for a few seconds at least, I was the only student within earshot.

I edged sideways in the hall, trying to get a view of the action inside the office.

"What's *obscene*, Reverend Bowd," Ms. Toles said evenly, "is the notion that teenagers should be kept purposely ignorant about the functioning of their own bodies!"

So it was Reverend Bowd who was getting Ms. Toles all bent out of shape. Frankly, I wasn't surprised. He was always raising a stink about something or other in town, and it usually involved sex. A year or so earlier, he'd organized this big protest when he'd learned that one of the local video stores carried X-rated movies.

"Corrine," Mr. Rall was saying, "I think Reverend Bowd may have a point about the cucumber. Maybe that was a tad graphic."

Suddenly, I knew what this little discussion was all about. A couple of weeks earlier, Ms. Toles had been telling her health classes how to use condoms, and she'd rolled one onto a cucumber (a *big* cucumber, or so I heard). It had been the talk of the school for a week or so, and now it seemed obvious that it had only been a matter of time until Reverend Blowhard got himself involved.

Ever so slowly, I'd inched myself to a point where I could actually see someone inside the office. It was Ms. Toles, all bony and freckled and pale. But she looked anything but frail. On the contrary, with her frizzy red hair and proud stance, she reminded me of a lion.

"It's well documented that the primary cause of condom failure among teenagers," Ms. Toles was saying, "is the fact that many kids don't know how to use them properly!"

I couldn't wait to hear what Reverend Blowhard would have to say to *that*! But then Mr. Rall appeared in the doorway, rumpled and sweaty and flushed. He was already closing the door when he happened to glance out into the hallway and see me.

He quickly jerked the door the rest of the way closed, but not before I saw the expression on his face. I don't think I've ever seen an adult look quite that scared before.

I knew I should've been excited later that day when Min and I sat down for lunch. After all, Kevin,

Terese, and Ike were meeting us, just like we'd agreed at the pizza parlor the day before. But instead of feeling excited, I felt uneasy about something—something I couldn't put my finger on. It wasn't quite one of those feelings of impending doom you get every now and then, but it was close.

Terese was the first to step up to our table.

"Hey," she said. She had her lunch in a greasy brown paper bag, but she didn't sit down.

"Hey!" I said, trying to sound all excited, despite how I felt. "Have a seat."

She looked both ways, like she was about to cross a busy street. Then she barreled straight ahead, pulled out a chair, and sat.

Min immediately looked down at her food. That's when it occurred to me that the two of them hadn't ever been seen together at school before. It had to be weird for them.

Ike came by next, sidling up to our table like a cat burglar trying to evade the police.

"Great," he said. "You guys made it." But he didn't sound like he thought it was great. He sounded like he sort of wished we'd forgotten.

Ike took a seat, but with an empty chair between him and everyone else.

We all sat there staring down at our food, and no one said anything, and I couldn't believe this was the same group of people from the day before. How could something that felt so comfortable then feel so awkward now? Then I remembered my second meeting with Kevin at the stinky picnic gazebo. That had felt uncomfortable too, with neither of us able to think of anything to say. That's when I knew that a conversation was like a child: you couldn't just abandon it, then pick it up again a day later and expect it to be exactly the way it was before.

But that was only part of it. This wasn't the back booth in a dark, deserted pizza parlor. This was the high school cafeteria. And in high school, everyone eats lunch with the same people every day. The people like them. Birds of a feather and all that? The four of us were birds of a feather, but no one knew that, and they couldn't ever know it.

Terese glanced over at the table of Girl Jocks, all sweatshirts and ponytails. Ike wasn't looking at the Lefty Radicals, with their piercings and Birkenstocks, but I could tell he knew they were there. It was like he wasn't looking at them on purpose, so they wouldn't notice where he was sitting.

Terese and Ike both knew they didn't belong at

Min's and my table. Min and I knew it too. How we all could've forgotten this, I don't know. We'd all been caught up in the excitement of the day before, and it had slipped our minds. But it had been in the back of my mind somewhere, because it was part of what had been bugging me, my feeling of semi-doom.

"'Sup?" It was Kevin, towering over us with his heaping tray of food and its three little cartons of milk. I breathed a sigh of relief. This was another thing that had been bothering me. I hadn't been sure Kevin was going to show. The day before, I'd been well aware that he was the only one of us who hadn't actually promised to come. But now that he *had* come, I wasn't sure if he was actually going to sit.

The funny thing was, I wasn't even sure I wanted him to sit there. It was one thing that Min, Terese, Ike, and I had sat down together. Maybe Terese's and Ike's friends would notice, but no one else would. It was something else entirely for Kevin Land to sit down with us. Everyone would notice that.

Kevin didn't sit. He didn't look nervous, but then I saw that he had such a firm grip on his tray that his knuckles were white.

"So," I said. "Here we are." You guessed it. The only thing I could think of to say.

This time, no one said anything, not even Min. Out of the corner of my eye, I saw Wendy Garr at the Girl Jocks table pointing over at Terese. Terese wasn't looking, but I knew she saw it too.

We were all having one of those "What were we thinking?" moments. What *had* we been thinking? Why hadn't we seen this coming? We were all citizens of different countries. Did we really think we could just pull up chairs and sit down together? There was no neutral territory on a high school campus. The land was all claimed, and the borders were solid. We couldn't just cross them at will.

The table two tables over was empty, and Brian Bund appeared out of nowhere and took a seat. He actually brought his lunch in a plastic lunchbox, and a *Buffy the Vampire Slayer* one at that.

Once again, I knew what we were all thinking. We were all thinking there were consequences for spending too much time outside the border of your own country. Eventually, they wouldn't let you back in. In other words, you ended up exiled and alone, like Brian Bund.

At that exact moment, Gunnar showed up. Min, Gunnar, and I had eaten lunch together forever. How I could've forgotten this too, I don't know.

"Hey," Gunnar said, his own tray in his hands and a hundred questions on his face.

"Gunnar?" I said.

"Gunnar!" Min said. She'd forgotten Gunnar too. But we couldn't very well turn him away, not without being total jerks. His arrival was actually good timing. It was the perfect excuse everyone needed to make their escapes.

Sure enough, Kevin said, "I should head. See you guys later!" I blinked, and he was walking away.

At exactly the same time, Terese gathered her food and stood. "Yeah!" she said. "Me too. Later!"

"Yeah!" Ike said, and he stood up so fast that he knocked over his chair.

Gunnar watched Kevin and Terese and Ike as they hurried away from us. Finally, he sat, still watching them as each was sucked back into his or her own circle of friends like a foreign particulate being engulfed by a giant white blood cell in some busy bloodstream.

"So," Gunnar said. "What was that all about?"

"Class project," Min said. Like me, she was a pretty good liar.

Even so, I didn't think Gunnar was buying. He'd spent his whole life trying to be popular, so he was keenly aware of the school's different cliques and groups. He knew what a strange gathering this had been. It didn't help that when he'd arrived, they'd all scattered like drug dealers from a bust.

"Hey," I said to Gunnar. "I've been getting woozy in algebra. They've been remodeling the classroom, and I think it's the formaldehyde in the pressboard." I was no fool. I knew when it was a good time to change the subject.

Sure enough, this time Gunnar took the bait. "It could be formaldehyde," he said. "Or it could be benzene or xylene. They're in pressboard too."

Gunnar kept talking, but I wasn't listening. I was thinking about Terese and Ike and Kevin (especially Kevin). I wasn't looking at any of them, and I knew none of them were looking at me. But once again, I knew exactly what they were all thinking. They were thinking what I was thinking, which was, Yesterday at that pizza parlor, I really made a connection with those guys. And now I wonder if I'll talk to any of them ever again.

## CHAPTER FIVE

But I did talk to them again, the very next day. We met after school deep in the stacks of the library. I wasn't sure whose idea it had been—I'd got the message from Min, who'd got an E-mail from Terese—but it was the perfect place to get together. If you're looking for solitude, a high school library is one of the best places to go, especially in the two hours after classes. And if anyone saw us, we could always pretend we weren't together, that we all just happened to be looking for a book in the same aisle at the same time.

Right before the meeting, I'd been wondering how it would feel. Would it be comfortable and real, like the pizza parlor? Or would it feel stilted and embarrassing, like the school cafeteria?

The second Min and I turned the corner and saw the faces of the others, I knew the answer. I felt that little swell of excitement like when you know you're about to set the top score on a well-used video game. Being one of the Nerdy Intellectuals I mentioned earlier, I generally like libraries anyway—I love the clean, heady musk of ink and paper and carpet glue. But I'd never been exhilarated in a library before. I was even glad to see Ike.

We all nodded our hellos, but I didn't look at Kevin, because I was thinking about what Min had said two days earlier, about him maybe liking me.

"Sorry about yesterday at lunch," Terese said, whispering.

Kevin and Ike mumbled their apologies too.

"It wasn't you guys' fault," I whispered back, and Min nodded. "It was no one's fault."

"Did your friends say anything?" Min asked Terese.

"Yeah," she said. "They wondered what was up."

"What'd you tell them?"

"That we were thinking about starting a club." She shrugged. "I'm a pretty good liar."

"What kind of club?" I said.

"I didn't say. I just changed the subject." So I wasn't the only one who avoided questions by changing the subject. Maybe this was another thing we all had in common.

"This is so stupid!" Ike said. "We shouldn't have to hide like this, like political dissidents or whatever. Why can't we be seen together like normal people?"

As if in answer, Candy Moon walked by the end of the aisle. I thought I saw her slowing down ever so slightly. Suddenly, this didn't seem like such a good meeting place after all. Five people in the same aisle was a pretty big coincidence.

"Damn," Kevin said, whispering again. "I think I had a bad idea, our coming here."

This meeting had been Kevin's idea? But why hadn't he E-mailed me directly? Did it mean Min was wrong, and Kevin didn't like me after all? Or did it mean just the opposite, that Min was right and he *did* like me, but that he was too shy to do anything about it? (Kevin Land shy? That was a laugh.)

"What we need," Min spoke softly, "is someplace to meet where no one'll see us."

"We could go back to the pizza place," Ike said. "We could meet there after school."

"No," Terese said. "Sooner or later, someone'll

see us. It's too close to school. The team goes there for pizza."

"Then some other restaurant," I said.

"I don't know," Kevin said. "Most nights, I got practice. It'd have to be close by. But like Terese said, if it's close to campus, we're gonna run into someone."

"The woods?" Terese said. There was this big forested area on the other side of the track field.

"Too cold and wet," Ike said.

"Wait a minute," Min said suddenly. "What Terese said. Why not start a real club?"

"Huh?" I said.

"You know," she said. "An after-school club. Don't they let you use a classroom? I mean, if you fill out the right forms?"

"What kind of club?" Terese said. She sounded suspicious. "You mean like a gay-straight alliance?" I'd heard about gay-straight alliances at other schools. Other big-city schools, that is. There were no gay-straight alliances in our town, maybe not even in our entire state, and there weren't going to be any anytime soon. If Reverend Blowhard could get so worked up over something as innocent as a teacher talking about contraceptives in a health class, it wasn't hard to imagine what he and his cadre of concerned parents would do over the existence of a gay-straight alliance at the local high school. The mushroom cloud would be visible for miles around.

"Well," Min said, "we don't need to tell anyone that's what kind of club it is. We'll just say it's a club."

"You have to," Ike said. "You have to say exactly what you are. They can't deny any club, not as long as you follow all the rules. My friends and me were going to start an Earth First! chapter, and Rall wasn't going to let us." (Remember, Mr. Rall was the school principal.) "But then Gladstein—he was our faculty advisor—he told Rall we'd sue if he didn't let us. Oh yeah, and you have to have a faculty advisor too."

No one said anything. We just thought about all the new information.

"Well, the first part is easy," I said. "We just make something up. We'll tell them it's a chess club when it's really just us."

"But what about the faculty advisor?" Ike said. "I mean, they'd be right there with us."

"Mr. Kephart," Min said.

We all looked at her.

"He's the most uninvolved teacher in the whole school! Two fifty-one in the afternoon, he's gone. If we ask him to be our advisor, the last we'll see of him is when he signs our application form."

"You think he'll do it?" Terese said.

"He will if I tell him he doesn't have to come to any of the meetings."

I felt a smile breaking out on my face. But at the same time, I saw movement at the end of the aisle. I turned to see Heather Chen staring right at us. Terese, Min, and I all snatched books from the shelves. It looked incredibly phony and probably made us look even more suspicious in Heather's eyes. When I looked back, she was gone.

"It's time to wrap this thing up," Min whispered, quieter than ever. "Are we all agreed about starting a club?"

"Hold on." Ike was barely whispering too. "There's still one more problem. If we start a club, it has to be open to every student in the school. That's the policy."

"Too bad we *can't* say it's a gay club," Terese said. "That'd keep everyone away." It was a joke, but it didn't sound like one, because she sounded so bitter.

Kevin hadn't said anything in a while, and I figured it was because he'd changed his mind and now he didn't want anything to do with this club thing. Or me.

So I was surprised when his face suddenly lit up, and he whispered, "I got it! We just choose a club that's so boring, nobody would ever in a million years join it!" He thought for a second. "We could call it the Geography Club!"

We all considered this. This time, I saw smiles break out all around.

The Geography Club, I thought. No high school students in their right minds would ever join that.

In other words, it was perfect!

"Trish Baskin's hot for you," Gunnar said to me.

It was the following Saturday, and Gunnar and I were playing racquetball on a court at the Y. I didn't completely suck at racquetball (that's my modest way of saying I was really pretty good). But Gunnar had said what he'd said about Trish Baskin right before his serve, so I had to wait until we finished the rally to ask him what the hell he meant. Of course, he won the point, but only because I was distracted.

"What?" I said.

"What what?" he said.

"What about Trish Baskin?" Our voices were echoing in the close confines of the brightly lit court.

"She does," Gunnar said. "I heard it from someone who knows. You like her?"

*Like* her? I thought. I barely even *knew* her. Oh, and then there was the small matter of my being queer as a three-dollar bill.

"She's okay," I said. She'd been in my geometry class the year before. She was sort of the mousy type, with this whispery voice and narrow shoulders and a streaked haircut that she'd probably had to be talked into getting. "Go ahead and serve."

"Well, she really likes you," Gunnar said, right before hitting the ball again. But I wasn't distracted this time, so I pounded it right past him and took back the serve.

We kept playing, and I noticed that Gunnar seemed quiet. Unlike Min, he wasn't particularly competitive, so I doubted he was thinking about the game. No, something else was going on here.

"Hey," he said a few minutes later, when he won back the serve.

I faced him, wiping my face with the sweat towel that had been hanging from my pocket.

He said, "Remember what we talked about a couple of weeks ago?"

I had absolutely no idea what he was talking about. "What do you mean?"

"You know. About my getting a girlfriend?"

Now I remembered. But he'd talked about that a zillion times before, so I still wasn't exactly sure where he was going with this.

"Yeah?" I said.

"Well, I think I got one. A girlfriend, I mean."

"Yeah? That's great! Who is it? Why didn't you tell me?" I was genuinely happy for him, in part because I wouldn't have to listen to him moan on and on about not having a girlfriend anymore.

"Kimberly Peterson."

"Gunnar, that's fantastic!" I said. "I'm really happy for you." I'd never actually spoken to Kimberly, but I'd seen her around school. She had long blond hair. That was about all I remembered, but keep in mind I don't exactly have a photographic memory when it comes to girls.

"Well, she's not really my girlfriend yet," Gunnar said. "But she did agree to go out with me."

"Well . . ." I tried to think of something positive to say. "I'm sure she'll like you once she gets to know you. Then she *will* be your girlfriend."

"Yeah," Gunnar said, tight-lipped, and I knew there was something he still wasn't telling me. Whatever it was, I had a bad feeling about it.

"Go ahead and serve," I said, and he did. I won the rally, but it was just plain luck. Now we were both distracted.

"Trish Baskin's *really* hot for you," Gunnar said. "She's friends with Kimberly. That's who told me."

I faced him. "Gunnar. What's going on?"

He was suddenly fascinated by the strings on his racquet. "Remember when we talked about my getting a girlfriend?"

I nodded.

"And remember when you promised you'd do anything to help me out?"

I nodded again, even though I didn't remember promising to do *anything* exactly.

"Well, Kimberly did agree to go out with me. But only on one condition."

"Oh," I said, and instantly I knew what was going on. "Gunnar, *no*!"

"Russ, why not? It'd only be one date!" Kimberly had agreed to go out with Gunnar only if I agreed to go out with her friend Trish, in case you haven't figured that out already.

"Gunnar!" My voice really echoed. I hadn't meant to yell.

"You said you'd do anything to help me!"

I was about to tell him exactly what I was thinking—that I hadn't said I'd do "anything" to help him. And even if I had, this wasn't what I'd meant! I'd meant driving with him to the mall so he could pick out a tux for the prom.

"Please, Russ. You know how important this is to me. Besides, it's just one date. What's the big deal?"

The big deal was I wanted to be dating Kevin Land! But I couldn't tell Gunnar that. Of course, putting up a big fuss about one little date with Trish Baskin was the next best thing to telling him. It was exactly the sort of thing that would make him suspicious.

I sighed. "It's a double, right? You and Kimberly and me and Trish?"

"Definitely!"

"When? Next weekend?"

Gunnar nodded. "Saturday."

I hesitated a second longer, just to make him squirm a little. Then I said, "Okay, I'll do it."

"Oh, thank God!" he said, far more relieved than he should've been.

"Gunnar," I said.

He still couldn't keep his eyes off those strings. "Yeah?"

"You already told Kimberly I'd do it, didn't you?"

He looked up at me at last, a tiny smile on his lips. "Maybe."

"Gunnar!"

But at least he had the decency to look properly ashamed about it, so I decided to let it slide.

"A date with a girl, huh?" Min said the next day, when I met her for a walk in the park. "That should be one hot and heavy evening."

"It sure wasn't my idea," I said. "You know her?"

"Trish? No. But I went to camp with Kimberly when I was eight. She used to eat paste, if that's any help. What does Gunnar like about her?"

"The fact that she has two X chromosomes." Min knew how much Gunnar wanted a girlfriend, and she laughed at my joke, which always made me feel good. You had to be pretty smart to make Min laugh.

"So," I said. "You excited about the Geography Club?"

"Yeah," Min said. But I noticed she'd suddenly stopped laughing, or even smiling.

"Where do you want to walk?" Min said, looking out over the hills of grass and bare trees. Winter was almost over, but there was a tinge in the breeze that hinted of a chill yet to come, like the smell of gunpowder in the air the week before the Fourth of July. The ground beneath our feet was cold and hard.

"Let's head for the Children's Peace Park," I said. This was a little garden on the other side of the park. There were shrubs and flowers, and in the middle of it all, there were these six painted wooden cutouts of the children of the world all holding hands. It was extremely stupid, but they'd put it up years before, when the Olympic torch had passed through town.

"What's up?" I said as we walked.

"Nothing," she said. She shrugged. "Terese."

"What?"

"I don't know. It's stupid. It's just . . ." She shivered, pulling her coat tighter around her neck. Min was chilly. "We got together last night at our warehouse."

"Yeah?"

"And things felt different."

I looked over at her. "What do you mean?"

She thought for a second. "Remember how I said Terese and I get together only in that warehouse?" I nodded. "No one ever saw us together, no one even knew about us. When we were together, it always felt like our own little world. This perfect, special place that only we could get to. It was like it wasn't quite real."

I nodded again, but secretly I was a little jealous. It sounded wonderful.

"But last night, it felt different," Min said.

"Because people know about you now? Kevin, Ike, and me?"

"I don't know. I guess. Nothing's really changed. But we got together at the warehouse last night, and it felt different. I still love her and everything. But it felt awkward. Like she wasn't quite the same person I remembered. Like we turned on the overhead lights in the warehouse, and we could see everything clearly for the first time, but nothing looked like we thought it did. Everything was messy. I liked it the way it was. I don't want light in that room."

"No one's going to tell," I said. "If you're thinking one of us is going to tell people about you guys, we won't." I don't know why I believed this so strongly— I barely knew Kevin and Ike. But I *did* believe it, as much as I'd ever believed anything. They'd never tell anyone about Min and Terese, and neither would I.

"It's not that," Min said. But she didn't say anything else, which made me think she didn't know what it was exactly. Finally, she said, "It's just a feeling."

"Maybe you just have to get used to it," I said. "People know now. I guess that makes it feel more real. But maybe once you get used to that, you'll go back to feeling the way you did before. Or maybe it'll be different, but better."

"Maybe," Min said, but I could tell she didn't believe me.

"You want to forget the idea of the club?"

"No. What's done is done." She said this hesitantly, but I was relieved anyway. Without Terese and Min, there was no Geography Club. And with no Geography Club, there was no Kevin and me.

"But?" I said.

"But I can't shake this feeling that something bad is going to happen."

I thought, Something bad to you and Terese, or something bad to the whole Geography Club? But I didn't ask this, because it seemed rude to be thinking of myself. Still, I couldn't help but remember what had happened the last time one of us had felt just a partial feeling of impending doom.

On that happy note, we reached the Children's Peace Park. It looked incredibly cheesy, just like I remembered. The painted wooden cutouts were all these horrible ethnic stereotypes of the children of the world. But it had been changed since I'd seen it last. Someone had taken a black marker and drawn tits on the wooden cutout of the Polynesian girl in the grass skirt, and they'd given the grinning, sombrero-wearing Mexican boy a hard-on. But the rosy-cheeked Eskimo boy had it worst. They'd pulled him off his base, kicked him in half, and knocked both pieces clean out of the garden.

"Nice," Min said.

"Yeah," I said, now shivering myself, and not just from the cold.

## CHAPTER SIX

"The first session of the Geography Club will come to order!" Kevin said in a voice that was a cross between television news anchor and Baptist preacher. Everyone laughed. He laughed too, but managed to add, "Damn! I knew I couldn't say that with a straight face!"

No one made the painfully obvious pun about none of us having "straight" faces, and I thought how glad I was to be here, surrounded by smart, funny friends, one of whom happened to be the hottest thing this side of an Old Navy commercial.

It was after school a few days later, and we'd gathered in an empty classroom on the second floor of the deserted school building. Technically, we weren't really the Geography Club yet—we hadn't been officially approved by the school. But we'd filled out all the necessary forms and submitted them to the school office, so it was only a matter of time. Mr. Kephart had agreed to be our faculty advisor, just like Min had said he would. And once he'd signed the forms, he'd disappeared from our lives forever, just like Min had said about that too. Before he'd headed for home, he'd even given us a key to his history classroom.

And so here we were.

Slowly, we all stopped laughing.

Here we go again, I thought. Another awkward silence, and I couldn't think of anything to say except, "So. Here we are," which had proved to be pretty worthless the last time around. There was a poster on the wall with a photograph of a bust of the head of Julius Caesar and a quote of something he said: "I came, I saw, I conquered." Whoever Julius Caesar had conquered, I knew how they felt. I felt defeated too. Was it going to be this hard to start a conversation every time we got together?

Kevin cleared his throat, and I thought, Oh, God, now Kevin's bored.

"We need rules," I blurted out.

They all looked at me.

"You know," I said. "Bylaws and stuff? It's not a geography club, but it's still a club."

I figured, if nothing else, at least this gave us something to talk about. I appreciated that no one flipped me any crap. Everyone was taking the club seriously.

"What kind of rules?" Terese said.

We all thought about it.

"How about we all get five minutes to say anything we want?" I said. "That's how we can start things out. We can kind of go around in a circle. And no one can interrupt." In the seventh grade, one of my classmates had been run over by a train. For the next couple of months, we'd had these support groups, and this is what the counselors had had us do. The Geography Club was a kind of support group, so I figured, What the hell?

Everyone nodded or grunted, which I guessed meant my motion had been carried.

Kevin said, "Whatever anyone says in this classroom stays in this classroom. No talking about the club with anyone outside." I figured this kind of went without saying—I'd said as much to Min that Sunday. But I was glad someone had said it anyway.

"Majority rules," Ike said. "If we ever have to

decide some issue, we take a vote. Whatever gets the most votes, we go with it. And since there are five members, we can't ever have a tie."

I couldn't imagine anything that we could possibly ever have to vote on, but it made sense in theory, so I nodded along with everyone else.

"How often do we meet?" Min said, and I realized this was the first thing she'd said in a long time. I couldn't help but remember what she'd said on Sunday, about the Geography Club screwing up her relationship with Terese, and I wondered what she was thinking. (Great, I thought: Now I didn't just have Kevin's every little reaction to worry about—now I had Min's to worry about too!)

"Twice a week?" I said in response to Min's question. This might sound like a lot of meetings, but being in high school, we had classes or workouts five days a week. So twice a week didn't seem that often.

"Which days?" Terese said.

What with Kevin's baseball games, Terese's soccer games, and Min's and Ike's other clubs, we had a hard time pinning down days. But we finally came up with Tuesday and Thursday, right after school. If we kept it at thirty minutes or so, Kevin and Terese could both get to their practices before the end of warm-up.

"Anything else?" I said. I meant any more rules.

We thought for a minute more, but no one came up with anything. They all looked at me, since for some reason I had suddenly become our unofficial leader.

"So I guess we get started with the five-minute thing," I said. Since it had been my idea, I figured it was up to me to go first. (Me and my big mouth!) I started in on everything that had been on my mind that day. Everything, that is, except Kevin and Min, the two things that had been most on my mind.

I wasn't exactly counting the minutes until the weekend and my date with Trish and Gunnar and Kimberly. Then Saturday morning rolled around, and I *did* start counting the minutes, but not in the good way. The truth was, I hadn't been on that many dates before. None, to be exact. Not real dates. Oh, I'd been to plenty of parties and group things, like when everyone gets together to go to a movie. But I'd never really done anything where I was paired up with one particular girl, and which involved the possibility of kissing or actual sex. (Do we really need to go into this again?) Let's just say that, up until this point in my life, I had kind of made it a point not to be alone with a girl.

Gunnar was picking me up at six, and then we were going to go pick up the girls at six thirty. So around four thirty, I started to get ready. I was allowing myself some extra time in case something went wrong, like if I cut myself shaving and had to be rushed to the emergency room so they could sew my nose back on.

I wasn't sure why I even cared what I looked like that night, but I did. So after I showered and combed my hair, I took a look at myself in the mirror. It's true, I had a whole flock of new zits on what was, three days ago, a blemish-free face. But I wasn't the worst-looking guy in the world.

Then I got dressed. I spent a good twenty minutes picking out the right pair of underwear to wear, turning sideways in the mirror and trying to decide which pair looked best. Again, I had no idea why. It's not like I thought there was any chance Trish would actually *see* me in them. It's also worth noting here that, as okay as I thought I looked, I looked nothing whatsoever like Kevin Land in a pair of Jockey shorts. Not that Kevin Land wore Jockey shorts. Kevin Land was a boxer shorts kind of guy. Which has absolutely nothing to do with my date with Trish, or even my getting ready for my date with Trish, so I'm not exactly sure why I'm going into it here. I guess just to give you some sense of exactly how much I was dreading this date.

Gunnar picked me up right on schedule, and I had to admit, he'd cleaned up well (smelled pretty good too). For one brief, very weird moment, I imagined it was the two of us going out on the date. The idea of dating Gunnar held absolutely no appeal, but the idea of being picked up in a car by a guy who'd taken a shower and put gel in his hair just for me—well, let's just say it appealed.

Trish was spending the night over at Kimberly's house, so Gunnar and I headed over there.

"Do you think we should get burgers after the movie?" Gunnar said to me, gripping the wheel as he drove. "Or maybe we should get pizza. We could eat at the food court at the mall, but they close at nine o'clock, so we'd have to eat first and go to the later movie, but I just had dinner, didn't you? Or we don't have to go to a movie. We could go to that teen dance club downtown. Do you think Kimberly would like that? But if we do that, we really won't be able to talk. Of course, we won't be able to talk at a movie either, but we could go out for food afterward; what do you think?"

There were a whole bunch of questions in there,

but I didn't answer any of them, because Gunnar never really stopped talking long enough, not even when we got almost to Kimberly's house. Obviously, Gunnar was even more nervous about this date than I was.

When we pulled up at Kimberly's house, Gunnar finally took a breath, so I turned to him in the front seat and said, "Gunnar? Calm down."

"What?" he said.

"Try to relax. You're making *me* nervous." Actually, this was a lie. The truth was, Gunnar's anxiety attack had somehow calmed me down. Go figure.

Gunnar took a couple of deep breaths, then nodded, and we headed for the flickering light of the front porch.

We'd barely pressed the doorbell when the front door flew open. It was Kimberly and Trish, filling the whole doorway. They both looked flustered, and there was a panicky look in Kimberly's eyes. Gunnar and I both took a couple involuntary steps backward on the porch.

Kimberly was already shouting back into the house. "I'm *leaving*!" she called. "'Bye, Mom; 'bye, Dad!" Then she glared at Gunnar and me, and said almost as loudly, "Go, go, *go*!"

Gunnar and I were both kind of speechless. But

Kimberly had already slammed the front door behind her and was now forcibly pushing us toward the car. "Come on, come on!" she said. "Let's *go!*"

Only now did I understand what was going on. Kimberly didn't want to have to introduce us to her parents. I didn't particularly want to be introduced to her parents, so this turn of events was fine with me.

Gunnar was clueing in at exactly the same time I was, so together, we all turned and bolted for the car like characters outrunning an explosion in an action-adventure movie.

Just as we reached the car, I saw a rectangle of light burst open on the front porch behind us. "Kimberly!" said the silhouette in the doorway. "Kimberly, wait a minute!" Kimberly's mom.

"Ignore her!" Kimberly whispered, throwing open two car doors at a time. "Let's just go!" She turned back toward the house and waved. "'Bye, Mom! We'll be home by one!"

"But Kimberly—!" the voice said, but it was too late. We were all inside the car now, and Kimberly's mom could only glower at us helplessly from within the wan light of the front porch.

"Drive!" Kimberly said, and Gunnar did. He didn't actually peel rubber, but he came close.

When we reached the end of the block, Kimberly finally relaxed, and the rest of us did too. Sitting in the front seat next to Gunnar, she lit up a cigarette. "Oh, man," she said. "There was, like, no *way* I was doing the whole parent thing."

"It's okay," Gunnar said. He hesitated a second, then added, "You need to change the bulb in your front porch light."

I thought, We've been on this date for ten seconds, and Gunnar has already said the wrong thing. This had to be some kind of new record.

Trish was sitting next to me in the backseat, so I turned to her and said, "Hey."

"Hey," Trish said. Up in the front seat, Kimberly was pretty heavily made up and was busting out all over in front. Trish, meanwhile, had a little less on her face and a little more on her body, but her clothes were pretty tight and didn't leave a whole lot to the imagination either. She didn't look horrible, though.

"You look great," I said, and she blushed.

"Thanks," she said in the mousy, whispery voice I remembered. "You do too."

"Where we headed?" Kimberly said, somehow managing to blow smoke in all our faces at exactly the same time.

"A movie?" Gunnar said. It was a question, not a statement, and I saw Kimberly wrinkle her nose in disgust. I knew right then that she liked her men loud and confident and crude, and that poor Gunnar didn't stand a chance.

We bought tickets for the stupid romantic comedy rated PG-13, but once we were inside the multiplex, Kimberly said she wanted to see the stupid erotic thriller rated R instead. As for me, I didn't want to see either the romantic comedy or the erotic thriller. I wanted to see the animated Disney musical, which I guess just proved that I really was the gay boy that I'd been thinking all along that I was. But once again, I knew enough to keep my opinion to myself, so we snuck into the erotic thriller just like Kimberly wanted.

There was a late-night entertainment complex in the same strip mall as the theater, and after the movie, we walked toward it across the parking lot.

"That movie was so gay," Kimberly said. She meant it sucked, and I hope it goes without saying that I was totally offended by this.

Then I noticed Gunnar looking at me in the dark, as if trying to read my reaction to Kimberly's comment about the movie. I thought, Why is he looking at me?

Does he have suspicions about me or what? But then it occurred to me that he was probably just trying to gauge my reaction to Kimberly, which was pretty thoroughly negative by this point.

Inside the entertainment place, Kimberly went off to play the pinball machines, with Gunnar trailing behind her and feeding her quarters as she went.

Trish and I went to the snack bar, where I ordered us a couple of burgers and Cokes.

"Kimberly's a lot of fun," I said as we stood around waiting for our food. I said this in a completely neutral way, so Trish wouldn't take offense if she really did think loud, obnoxious Kimberly was a lot of fun. But I really meant it sarcastically, and I figured Trish would pick up on it if she thought the same thing.

"Oh, she's okay," Trish said. "She just gets like that when she has too much to drink." Kimberly had brought a flask into the theater and had been slipping rum into her Coke all during the movie. Of course, this didn't explain her being a bitch even *before* the movie, but I didn't point this out to Trish.

Once we picked up our food, we headed for a booth, and I noticed that a couple of guys were checking Trish out. (Like I said, her clothes were pretty tight.) They both looked at Trish, their eyes scanning her like an X-ray machine. Then finally they looked at me, and I knew what they were thinking. They were jealous. This was all new to me, so I didn't quite know what to do here. Should I bare my teeth and growl?

"How long you guys been friends?" I said to Trish once we'd started in on our food.

"Forever," Trish said. "Since first grade."

"Like Gunnar and me. We met in the fourth grade."

"She's really not that bad once you get to know her."

I had a mouthful of food, but I spoke up anyway. "What makes you think I think she's bad?"

Trish just smiled knowingly. "I can tell." Maybe I hadn't been as neutral as I'd thought when I'd said that about Kimberly being a lot of fun. Or maybe Trish was just perceptive.

"I'm glad you came tonight," Trish said.

"Yeah?" I said.

"Yeah. I liked when we had that class together last year. I liked talking to you."

"Yeah? Me too." The truth was, I barely remembered talking to her, and I sure hoped Trish wasn't so perceptive that she could see this too.

Suddenly, Kimberly appeared, desperate for us to

join her in a game of House of the Dead II.

There's not too much more to tell about the date. We finished eating, then played video games, then ate some more. By then, Kimberly was feeling kind of sick, so Gunnar and I drove the girls home, and he walked Kimberly to the front door, and I said good-bye to Trish at the car. This was so we could all kiss each other good night and not have it seem like some kind of orgy.

"Thanks," I said to Trish, standing in the glare of a streetlight that totally blotted out the moon. "I really had a good time."

"Yeah," Trish said, sidling closer. "Me too."

Then we kissed. Her face was in shadow, so our mouths kind of missed at first. But then we made contact. Her lips were warm and squishy, like overcooked asparagus, and it freaked me out a little. But at least there were no tongues involved.

Trish pulled away first. "Call me?" she said.

"Definitely," I said. You weren't actually supposed to tell the truth here, were you?

Then she was running up to the front porch, crossing paths with Gunnar, who was on his way back to the car.

Okay, so maybe I wasn't the best date in the world.

But at least this stupid thing with Trish was over and done with.

Or so I thought.

That Monday morning, I walked into school and was greeted by the ring of echoing voices, the smell of perfume and soda pop, and the sight of people standing around in tight little clusters reading copies of the *Goodkind Gazette*.

Wait a minute, I thought. Something about this picture was wrong. No one *ever* read the school newspaper.

What was worse, all around me, people weren't just talking; they were buzzing with excitement. Here it was before eight o'clock on a Monday morning, and people were acting like it was afternoon on the last day before Christmas vacation. But I couldn't make out anything that anyone was saying—it was just one long, reverberating rumble.

I glanced at the closest group of people. Sure enough, two of them were reading an article on the front page of the *Goodkind Gazette*. Both of them looked absolutely enraptured by what they were reading, like it revealed both the secrets of the universe and the answers to this afternoon's biology test. Everyone else must have already read the article, because they were all yammering on, sometimes making these wild gestures to the newspaper itself.

I still couldn't make out what was being said, but suddenly, for no reason I can explain, one word happened to rise above the din.

"Banana," said Tad Brickle.

People were excited about an article in the *Goodkind Gazette* about a banana? This was getting stranger and stranger.

I drifted closer to the closest cluster of people and tried to read the headline of the article over the shoulder of Brittany Vanderberg. But just then she turned the page to where the article continued on page two.

Then I overheard another word.

"Toles," said Monica Melnacht.

Toles? I thought. As in Ms. Toles, the health teacher? For some reason, this made me nervous.

I turned for a nearby newspaper dispenser, but it was empty. That was a first too.

This is just stupid, I thought. I should just walk up and ask someone what all the commotion is about.

That's when I heard Zack Ward say the word "gay."

Gay? People were reading about something "gay"

in the school newspaper? I didn't like the sound of that at all!

I hurried to Min's locker, hoping she could fill me in.

"What's going on?" I said when I found her.

She glanced around us in the hallway, seeing if the coast was clear. "We're screwed," she said under her breath. "That's what's going on."

"Who is?"

"The Geography Club." I hadn't thought I could get any more tense, but I did just then.

"What?" I said. *Why?*

She pulled a copy of the newspaper from her locker and presented it to me like a teacher handing me a pop quiz. "Read it," she said.

I didn't want to read it. I wanted Min to tell me what was going on!

"Just tell me!" I said.

"Ms. Toles gave an interview to the school paper."

So what if the health teacher gave an interview to the *Goodkind Gazette*? What could that possibly have to do with the Geography Club?

"So?" I said. I sounded impatient, but the truth was, now I wasn't so sure I wanted to know.

"So *read* it!" Now Min sounded impatient too.

I snatched the newspaper from her hand. Min pointed to the article, and I started reading.

The headline was "Health Teacher Speaks Her Mind, Makes Controversy." Now I know what people mean when they say their heart is in their throat.

It was a profile of Ms. Toles. It talked about her feelings on sex education and how she felt about condom machines in high school bathrooms (she was for them) and "abstinence-only" curriculums (she was against them). It also talked about when she'd put those condoms on that cucumber in class. ("Not one single student complained to me about that," Ms. Toles said, "and after those classes, three students came up to thank me." I had to admit these were pretty good points.)

I didn't need to finish the article to know that Ms. Toles was toast. She'd have been gone by the end of the year with just the cucumber and the condoms. Now with this article in the paper, she'd be gone in a week. I couldn't help but wonder what in the world she'd been thinking.

But none of this had anything to do with Geography Club, or anything "gay," and I couldn't figure out why Min was so upset.

"What?" I said. "I don't see any—"

"Turn the page," Min said, "and keep reading!"

I yanked open the page—partly tearing it in the process—and kept reading.

Two paragraphs before the end of the article, I came to a line that made my blood run cold. It was a quote from Ms. Toles.

"'As a health educator, it's my job to teach all the students,' Toles said.

"According to Toles, that even includes gay students. 'There are gay and lesbian students at every high school in town, including ours,' Toles said. 'Just last week, I talked to one of them about a support group for gay teens.'"

Talk about burying the lead! This is what everyone had been chattering about in the hallways. This was also why Min was so upset. Someone had spilled the beans about the Geography Club!

## CHAPTER SEVEN

Terese was pissed. "All right!" she demanded. "Who talked?"

It was that same Monday after school, at an emergency meeting of the Geography Club. Terese wasn't the only one angry about that article on Ms. Toles. No one had even said hello. The five of us had just stomped into the classroom and gathered in a circle, glowering at each other like competitors in a game of tag-team wrestling.

When no one stepped forward to admit guilt, Terese said, *"Well?"* She meant business, but then so did everyone else.

"It wasn't me," I said, if only because we needed

to start the ball rolling somehow.

"Terese," Min said, "you know it wasn't me."

Ike shook his head. "I never even talked to Toles before."

Terese whirled on Kevin. "Then it had to be—!"

Kevin held up his hands and sort of ducked, like he thought Terese was going to hit him. "Wait a minute!" Kevin said. "It wasn't me either!"

"Then *who*?" Terese said.

We were back to standing there scowling at each other like a pack of fur-bristled wolves.

Then something occurred to me. "Terese?" I said.

Now she turned on me. *"What?"*

"It's just that you're the only one who didn't—"

She gave me one seriously droll look. "No! It wasn't me either."

Min sat down at one of the desks. She looked as confused as I felt. Ike started pacing. And Kevin had slipped a baseball from his backpack and was squeezing it and tossing it ever so lightly into the air. I'd never seen him do this before, but I knew right away that this was a nervous habit. (Even upset like I was, I found this endearing.)

"It really wasn't anyone here?" Terese said.

"It wasn't me," Min said.

"Or me," I said.

"Or me," Kevin said.

"It wasn't me," Ike said.

I looked from person to person, at the droop in their shoulders and the hangdog expressions on their faces. I believed them. Suddenly, I was certain that no one in that room had squealed. Everyone else was beginning to believe it too. We'd already said too much of the truth to each other to start lying now. As we kept looking back and forth at each other, I could feel the tension start to drain from the room.

"Then who?" Terese said quietly.

Min looked up suddenly. "Well, who says it was one of us? There are eight hundred students at this school. There have to be more than five gay people. Maybe it was one of them."

"Oh yeah!" Terese said. "And they just happen to be starting a gay support group at the same time we are?"

"Hold on," I said. "Toles didn't actually say they were starting a gay support group. She just said they talked about a support group for gay teens."

We all thought about this for a second.

"So no one talked," Terese said. She sounded both grateful and relieved.

"Pretty bad timing, though," Ike said. "I mean, with our club and everything. Everyone's talking about the gay club and who the gay kid might be."

"So what?" Min said suddenly. "We don't have anything to worry about. I mean, no one here's going to talk, so how could anyone find out? We're the Geography Club. It's official! Why would anyone ever suspect us?"

We all thought about this too. It did make some sense.

"People already think they know who the gay kid is," Ike said. "My friends do anyway."

"Yeah," Kevin said. "Mine too."

"Me too," Terese said.

"I've been hearing things," Min said.

"Who do people think it is?" I said, as if I didn't know.

Sure enough, Ike said, "Brian."

Kevin said, "Brian."

Terese said, "Brian."

And Min said, "Brian."

I thought, Who says the different cliques and groups at our school don't have anything in common? They all seemed pretty united in their hatred of Brian Bund. The poor kid. Like he really needed people to be even more evil to him.

"So no one's even going to suspect us?" Terese said, and Min nodded.

We were quiet a second longer, then Kevin said, "Docious!" This was short for "supercalifragilistic- expialidocious," from that movie *Mary Poppins*, and it's an example of my generation's famous ironic wit. It's sort of an all-purpose word at our school that can mean something is really good ("hot damn!") or really bad ("holy shit!"). Kevin just meant he was glad that nothing bad had happened to the Geography Club.

In fact, Kevin was so glad, he wasn't nervously flipping his baseball anymore. Now he was happily tossing it high into the air. But on the way down, he misjudged his catch and accidentally tipped the ball away from his body. I happened to be standing next to him, so I reached out and snatched the baseball just before it hit the ground.

"Good catch!" Kevin said as I tossed him back the ball. "You ever think about joining the baseball team?"

I hadn't ever thought about it. But I did now.

I was surprised to see that Gunnar had waited for me during the meeting of the Geography Club. I found him reading on the grass by the bike racks. This was dedication, since it was still pretty cold outside. Either that, or he wanted something from me.

"Hey," he said, standing and packing his book away. "Where you been?"

"Oh," I said. "Sorry. I joined a club. Normally, our meetings are Tuesdays and Thursdays, but we had a special meeting today."

"What kind of club?"

This was the question I'd been dreading from Gunnar for days. If anyone in our whole school would be interested in joining something called the Geography Club, it would be Gunnar. He was just that strange.

"It's called the Geography Club," I told him. "But it's really boring. I'm just doing it to have something to put on college applications."

"Oh." I expected him to ask me questions about it, but he didn't. "So, you ready to ride?"

"Yeah, sure." I started unlocking my bike, but what I really wanted to do was jump up and knock my heels together and shout, "Gunnar doesn't want to join the Geography Club!"

We climbed on our bikes and started for home.

"So," Gunnar said. "You have a good time on Saturday?"

It took me a second to realize he was talking about

my date with Trish. Since the date had ended, I'd given Trish pretty much no thought whatsoever.

"Yeah," I said. "Trish is nice." I knew Gunnar had to feel pretty bad about his date with Kimberly. There was no reason to make him feel worse for having set me up with Trish. Besides, my date really hadn't been that bad. "Sorry it didn't work out with you and Kimberly," I said.

"Who says it didn't work out?" Gunnar said. He sounded offended.

I had to look at him to see if he was making a joke. It looked like he really *was* offended.

"What?" I said.

"What what? What makes you think it didn't work out with Kimberly?"

"Well, I . . ." I thought back on what Gunnar and I had talked about on Saturday night after we'd dropped off the girls. Neither of us had ever said outright that his date with Kimberly had been a complete and utter disaster. But Kimberly had been such a bitch in general, and she'd seemed so indifferent to Gunnar all night long, that I'd just assumed he knew it had been a disaster. The only reason I hadn't said anything Saturday night was because I didn't want to make him feel any more miserable than I assumed he already did.

"What are you saying?" I said. "You still like Kimberly?"

"Sure! She likes me too. We talked today in free period. She wants to go out again this weekend."

"What?" I knew it was rude to sound so shocked, but I couldn't help myself. I just couldn't believe that Kimberly actually wanted to go out with Gunnar again. Was he making this up?

"You sound surprised," Gunnar said.

I tried to pretend that the astonishment in my voice was just me huffing from riding my bike. "No," I said. "No! That's great. I mean, you like her, right?"

"You don't?"

"I didn't say that!" Why did everyone keep thinking I didn't like Kimberly? It was true, but why did everyone keep thinking it?

"So she got a little drunk," Gunnar said. "She was just having fun."

I was torn. Part of me was happy for Gunnar. I knew how much he wanted a girlfriend. But another part of me thought, God, does it have to be that bitch Kimberly Peterson? She couldn't possibly end up being any good for him. How could she be? She didn't even seem to *like* Gunnar. She was probably just using him for something—but what?

"Oh," I said, because suddenly I knew exactly what she was using him for.

Kimberly may not have liked Gunnar, but Trish liked me. That's what Kimberly's second date with Gunnar had to be all about. Trish wanted to go out with me again. Since they knew that Gunnar liked Kimberly—that was pretty screamingly obvious—Kimberly was stringing Gunnar along in hopes he, as my best friend, would use his influence to get me to go out with Trish again. Or maybe Trish just didn't want to go out alone with me yet—maybe she wanted Kimberly and Gunnar along one more time. Either way, I knew in my gut that my going out with Trish was the only reason Kimberly was willing to go out with Gunnar. If I refused to go on another date with Trish, Kimberly would dump Gunnar's ass.

"'Oh,' what?" Gunnar said.

"It's just . . ." I started to say what I was thinking. But then I looked over at the guy on the bike next to me, and I saw the look on his face. He had one of those open, completely vulnerable expressions that made me just know if I said the truth, he would never look quite that innocent ever again.

That's when I decided he didn't need to know the truth. Besides, maybe I was wrong. What did I know? Maybe Kimberly did like Gunnar. He did have kind of a geeky charm. I was the first to admit I didn't know how these crazy straight people did their dating thing. (I didn't know how we crazy gay people did our dating thing either, but that was a whole other story.)

"Oh, there's more good news!" Gunnar said, but I already knew what it was: Trish wanted to go out with me again too.

"What?" I said.

"Trish wants to go out with you again too," Gunnar said. "Kimberly thought we could double again." He tried to make this sound exciting, but I could hear the worry in his voice, the fear that I was going to put up another big fuss about going out with Trish, just like I had the first time. In other words, on some level, I think even Gunnar knew he was just being used.

"Well?" Gunnar said.

I mustered up the biggest grin I could for my friend. "That sounds great. I'd love to take Trish out again!"

It was just one more little date. How bad could it be?

The next day before school, I met Min by her locker and told her that I had yet another date with Trish Baskin. Without making myself sound too noble, I also told her why.

She smiled in an admiring kind of way. Then she said, "You're a really nice guy. You know that, Russel? You're a thoroughly decent guy."

I blushed a little. Even more than making Min laugh, I liked making her think I was decent. I guess because I thought she was decent too.

I stepped closer to her in the hallway and lowered my voice. "So how's it going? With Terese, I mean."

She didn't seem to know what I was talking about, which I thought was a little weird. She said, "What do you mean?"

"Well," I said, "last week in the park you sounded pretty bummed."

"Oh, that." She rolled her eyes. "That was just me being stupid."

"Really?"

"Yeah. We've gotten together a couple times since

then. Nothing's changed. Or if it has, it's better."

"Really?"

She nodded. This was no brave face she was putting on. She was telling the truth.

"Well, that's great!" I said.

I thought about all that had happened in the last day or so. Min and Terese were back to being good. It turned out no one had spilled the beans about the Geography Club. And Kevin wanted me to join the baseball team. True, I was gay and I was dating a girl— and one I didn't particularly like at that. But I was doing it for a friend, so it didn't seem like such a whopping big deal.

The fact is, things were finally going right, and I couldn't imagine anything that could possibly change that.


"That's it, Middlebrook!" Kevin Land said to me. "Now I'm gonna mop the floor with your face!"

It was that afternoon at the Tuesday meeting of the Geography Club and we were playing baseball in Kephart's classroom. We were using a Ping-Pong ball for a ball and an eraser for a bat. Kevin was pitching, and I was up to bat. It was Kevin and Terese against

Ike and Min and me.

"Hey, batter, batter!" Terese intoned. "Hey, batter, batter!"

Kevin pitched, and I swung. There was a very satisfying *thwap*, and the ball went flying up over the desks.

"Run!" Min shouted to me. *"Run!"*

I didn't need to be told. I was already off and running for first base, which happened to be a desk in the front row of the classroom.

"Get it, get it!" Kevin shouted to Terese. "Throw it here!" But it was clacking wildly under the desks in the back of the room, and she was having a hard time pinning it down.

"Go!" Min said to me. "Keep going!"

When I reached first, Terese was still fumbling for the ball, so I took off for second base—another desk.

"Come on!" Ike shouted. "Bring it home!"

Soon I was rounding third, and there was still no Ping-Pong ball in sight.

"Hurry!" Kevin yelled to Terese. *"Hurry!"*

"I got it!" Terese said, standing bolt upright. She threw it to Kevin, who snatched it from the air and rushed to meet me at home plate. He crashed into me with the force of a meteor—a meteor with biceps and a six-pack!

"Out!" Kevin said, his arms wrapped tightly around me.

"Safe!" Ike said.

"Out!" Terese said.

*"Safe!"* Min said.

"Safe!" I said. "Three against two!"

"Boooooo!" Terese yelled from the back of the classroom. "Cheap call, cheap call!"

We all started laughing, and I honestly couldn't think of another time when I'd felt so close to a group of people. (Did I mention that Kevin had his arms wrapped tightly around me?)

Just then, someone knocked on the door to our classroom.

"Oops," Terese said, her eyes widening in mock horror. "Too loud."

We all stifled our smiles as best we could (and Kevin pulled away from me at last), and Min went to answer the door.

"Yeah?" she said.

It was a large black girl in a bright orange sweater with a matching orange headband in her hair. She was a junior, and a member of the orchestra, which put her somewhere between the Computer Geeks and the Lefty Radicals in terms of popularity (closer to the Computer Geeks).

"Is this the Geography Club?" she said.

"Yeah," Min said. "Sorry if we were a little loud."

"It's not that," said the girl.

"Then what?"

"Well, I wanted to know how I would go about joining."

## CHAPTER EIGHT

"Join *what?*" Min said to the fat girl with the orange headband in her hair. It was just seconds after she'd interrupted our game of classroom baseball.

The girl in the doorway tilted her head. "Well, the Geography Club. Didn't you say that's what this was?"

"You want to join the Geography Club?" Ike said.

She nodded.

No one said anything, and I felt my stomach plunging like a brakeless elevator. A nongay student wanted to join the Geography Club? If we turned her away, we couldn't stay an after-school club and could no longer use Kephart's classroom, which basically meant the end of the Geography Club. But if we let her join, we could no longer talk about the things we wanted to talk about—we'd have to talk about actual *geography*!—and that meant the end of the Geography Club too.

"Why?" Terese said to the girl. It was the same thing we were all thinking.

"Why what?" said the girl.

"Why the Geography Club?"

The girl shrugged, and I noticed she was wearing yellow smiley-face earrings. "I figured it'd help me on my college tests," she said. "I'm Belinda Sherman, by the way."

"There is no geography on the SAT," Min said.

"There isn't?" Belinda said. "Well, it can't hurt, right?"

"But geography's *boring*," Kevin said, almost indignant.

"Well, isn't that the point of the club? To make it less boring?" Belinda Sherman wasn't just not gay—she was bubbly. I hated bubbly. I hated bubbly even more than I hated bitchy à la Kimberly Peterson.

"How'd you find out about us?" I asked.

"Oh, I saw your application. I do work-study in the school office."

"There's a fifty-dollar equipment fee!" Terese said.

"You know, for maps and atlases and stuff?"

"Oh," Belinda said. She thought for a second. "I bet my uncle'll pay. He's a carto-whatever? He makes maps. Actually, he's just a surveyor, but it's kind of the same thing. Maybe he can come in and talk to us sometime, huh?"

We were speechless. What was there to say? Belinda, a bubbly high school junior with an orange headband and smiley-face earrings, had come, she'd seen, and she'd conquered.

The next day, I joined the baseball team.

I wish I could say I joined because I wanted to play baseball and that I'd been thinking about it for a long time. But I can't say that, because I didn't and I hadn't. The truth was, I thought baseball was kind of boring. And I dreaded the thought of spending even more time every day in a locker room full of bone-headed, swaggering jocks.

No, the bottom line was I joined the baseball team because Kevin asked me to. That and the fact that the addition of Belinda Sherman to the Geography Club basically meant the *end* of the Geography Club. I thought, If I don't join the baseball team, I'll never see Kevin again. It was an exaggeration, but it made sense at the time. (What can I say? I was a fool in love.)

So the minute the school bell rang at the end of classes, before I could talk myself out of it, I aimed myself for the gym and its all-purpose locker rooms. I beat all of the baseball players and other athletes who used the locker room that time of year. The baseball coach was also a P.E. teacher, and I knew I'd find him in the little coach's office just off the locker room.

I knocked on the door, and he answered. He was bald and fat, which I thought was kind of ironic for a gym teacher.

"I want to join the baseball team," I said.

"Yeah?" he said, perking up. "Where you play before?"

I told him I hadn't really played baseball since the seventh grade, and he got noticeably less excited after that. But I *had* played baseball in the seventh grade, and I hadn't completely sucked. (Remember, this means I was actually pretty good.) And I'd been pretty good in that game of classroom baseball too.

"What position you play?" the coach said.

Position? I thought. I didn't know I needed to play a particular position. In the seventh grade, we'd all kind of rotated.

"Shortstop," I said, because it was the first thing

that popped into my head.

Then he gave me a list of the equipment I'd need, including some embarrassing jock things that I wasn't looking forward to buying again. And he gave me a form I'd need filled out by my doctor and parents, and sent me on my way.

I hadn't even left the locker room when all my doubts about joining the team crashed down on top of me. I'd almost certainly make a fool of myself. Besides, it was so stupid to be doing all this just for Kevin's sake. Didn't I have any pride?

But on my way out of that locker room, I ran into Kevin himself on his way to practice.

"Hey," I said, trying not to sound too excited. "I just joined the team."

"Team?" he said.

"Baseball."

Kevin gaped at me for a second. Then he said, "Docious! Hey, we sure can use the help!" The longer he spoke, the wider his grin became. I could almost see myself in the white enamel of his teeth.

And suddenly, I didn't care that I didn't know my baseball "position," or that deep down I knew that joining a team just to be close to a guy was basically a really bad idea.

Kevin Land was happy I'd joined the baseball team, and that was all that mattered!

Was I pathetic or what?

That weekend, I had my second date with Trish Baskin.

Gunnar drove me and him to Kimberly's house, where Trish was once again spending the night. At least this time, we didn't have to outrun Kimberly's parents. This time, Gunnar had arranged to meet the girls on the corner at the end of the block. For the first time in my life, I was the kind of guy a girl snuck out of her house at night to meet (except I wasn't really).

We went to dinner at a Chinese restaurant, and Kimberly wanted everything deep-fried, so everything that could be deep-fried was deep-fried.

Halfway through the meal, she said, "There's a fucking *hair* in the hot-and-sour soup!"

"I think that's *your* hair," I said to her. I sure didn't see anyone working in the restaurant with long blond hair.

"Shut the fuck up!" Kimberly said. "You wanna get this meal for free or not?"

In other words, Kimberly was her usual charming self.

When we were through eating, Gunnar and I paid the bill. (Not only didn't I want the meal for free, I left a big tip, to make up for Kimberly being so loud and annoying all through dinner.)

Afterward, we headed for the teen dance club downtown. I'd never been before, and the raccoon in me was impressed by the mirrors and the flashing lights. The music was blasting, which made it impossible to talk, but given that I was with Trish and Kimberly, this wasn't necessarily a bad thing.

Gunnar and Kimberly went off to get drinks, and I leaned over to Trish. "This place is something else," I said, almost a shout.

She nodded and said something in response, but I had no idea what it was, because she was still talking in that soft, whispery voice of hers.

"You want to dance?" I said, and Trish nodded.

After five or six songs, Trish leaned toward my ear, and this time I did hear her, if only barely. "Wanna go for a drive?" she said. "Just the two of us."

A drive? I thought. We'd just gotten there, and I'd just dropped twenty bucks getting us both inside. Why did she want to go for a drive?

"How?" I said. "We don't have a car."

"You can borrow Gunnar's."

I shrugged. "I'll go ask him."

When I found Gunnar and told him why I wanted to borrow his keys, he looked confused.

"What?" I said.

"Nothing," he said, quickly palming me the keys before scooting off to find Kimberly, who'd somehow evaded him. He seemed tweaked about something.

Trish and I got our hands stamped, then left the club. It had started raining while we were inside. It wasn't quite a downpour, but by the time we reached the car, I was pretty wet. It was cold out too, but I was still sweaty from dancing, so I barely felt it.

Once inside the car, I said, "Where'd you wanna go?"

"Oh, I didn't have any place in mind," she said.

So I drove to this long stretch of park along the water just north of downtown.

"Hey," Trish said. "Let's stop the car." From where we were, there's usually a pretty good view of the islands across the bay. But it was dark, and the falling rain looked like gray sheets blowing in the wind, so you could just barely make out the black out-lines of the land across the water.

I pulled over, and we sat in silence for a minute or two. Except for the rain tapping on the roof and sliding down the windshield, everything was completely still. With the commotion of the dance still ringing in my ears, the quiet seemed unnerving. By now, we'd also cooled down a bit. The heater hadn't been on long enough to warm up the car, and it was chilly.

"That club is something else," Trish said.

"Yeah," I said, thinking, Hadn't I said the same thing to her just an hour earlier?

We sat side by side in that seat for a long time. Finally, Trish shivered and pulled her jacket tighter around her.

"Are you cold?" I said, reaching for the ignition. "I can turn—"

"No," Trish said. "I'm okay. I just . . ." Without warning, she slid over in the seat until she was pressed against me. Then she slipped her arms around me and buried her face against my chest. I raised my arm to get it out of the way, and Trish looked up, took hold of it, and placed it around her shoulders.

"There," she said contentedly. "That's *much* better."

We sat like that for a couple of minutes, a human tangle. I felt stiff and awkward, but I didn't dare move for fear of bumping or jostling Trish.

"I can hear your heartbeat," Trish said, her voice muffled.

"Oh," I said. I could hear my heartbeat too. It was pounding in my ears.

There was another silence. I was sweating again, despite the cold inside the car. I wasn't an idiot. I knew the final destination of this little "drive" of hers. But I couldn't just shove her off me, now, could I?

"Russel?" Trish said.

"Yeah?" She was looking up at me, but I didn't look down at her.

"Do you like me?" she said.

What were you supposed to say to a question like this? I lied and said, "Yeah."

"'Cause I like *you*."

"Great."

"Russel?"

When she didn't say any more, I peeked down at her at last. Her eyes were closed and her lips were kind of puckered, and I knew she wanted me to kiss her.

Gunnar, I thought, I am going to kill you! But the only way out of this horrible evening was through it. Despite the fact that her breath reeked, I leaned down and kissed her.

The second my lips touched hers, Trish's mouth

slid open like a garage door on rollers, and I felt her tongue poking up between my lips. It felt like a raw oyster with a mind of its own. In my surprise, I lifted my mouth away.

Trish's eyes popped open. "What's wrong?" she said.

I clawed limply at the car door. "I don't know. Nothing. I just don't think we should . . . "

"What?"

"You know."

"Why not?"

"Well, we don't have any condoms."

Trish pulled back and sat upright next to me on the seat.

"Well, I didn't say I wanted to have *sex* with you, now, did I? I thought we were just kissing!"

"Oh." I felt like a fool. But at least I'd managed to stop the kissing.

Trish hesitated. Then she whispered, even quieter than usual: "But if you *did* want to, I've got some in my purse."

I stared out at the rain, which was really beginning to come down. So even Trish the Mouse had sex. And now she wanted it with me. How the hell had I ended up in this mess? More important, was there any way out?

"You haven't done it before," Trish said. "Have you?"

"What?" I said, shocked and appalled. "Yes! I've done it!"

"When? With who?" Suddenly, Trish wasn't talking in a whisper anymore. It was strange to hear what her real voice sounded like at last.

"You sound like I'm on trial," I said. "This girl on my block." This was a complete lie. There was no girl. There never would be any girl, not if I could help it.

"It's okay if you haven't. It's no big deal."

I didn't say anything.

"What?" Trish said. "Are you gay or something?"

"No! Of course not!" Obviously, another lie.

We sat there for a minute more, both of us looking at the rain swirling down the windshield. Ordinarily, when you heard raindrops on the roof above you, you were supposed to say how you were glad you weren't out in that. But I would much rather have been out in that rain than inside that car with Trish.

"So," Trish said. "You want to or what?"

"What?" I said, even though I knew damn well what.

She turned to me and smiled. "You know."

"Oh," I said.

Trish kept staring at me, and I still couldn't think of any way out. If I turned her down, Trish would tell everyone all about it. And there was only one kind of guy who turned a girl down. People could do the math.

"Just relax," she said, scooting closer again. "Okay?" I felt her hands on me, and she started kissing me again. Her tongue slipped back inside my mouth, and I immediately thought of that creature in the *Alien* movies, the one that attaches itself to your face and crams itself down your throat so it can implant an embryo in your stomach.

No, I thought. This was too much. If I went through with this, then I really wouldn't have any dignity. Suddenly, I didn't care what Trish told people about me. I pushed her away. Kind of hard, I guess.

"Huh?" she said, jerking upright. "What's wrong?"

"Nothing," I said. "I just think we should get back to the dance."

Trish sighed, as if in defeat, and fell back against the back of the seat.

"It's not you!" I said quickly. "It's just . . . you were right. I'm, like, you know, a virgin. And I always thought my first time would be different. Special, I guess. Not in the front seat of a car. I really like you, but if we ever do this, I think it should be special." Even I, a pretty accomplished liar, was surprised at how easily this latest lie came to me, and how convincing it sounded. But I'd needed a good lie to keep Trish from knowing the real reason I was pushing her away.

Fortunately, Trish's face began to melt. "Oh! Russel, that's okay. It's really sweet actually. We don't have to tonight. And you're right. Your first time *should* be special."

After that, Trish agreed we should head back to the teen dance club. With all my sweating, the ink stamp on my hand was almost completely gone. But they remembered me, so they let me back in.

We found Gunnar and Kimberly, and Trish and Kimberly immediately headed off to the bathroom, where I knew Trish was telling Kimberly all.

"Okay," Gunnar said to me while we waited. "What happened?"

"What?" I said.

"With Trish! You went for a 'drive'?"

"Nothing happened! We talked."

I could tell Gunnar didn't believe me. He was certain we'd fooled around. I wasn't surprised that was what he thought. As a master liar, I knew people believed what they wanted to believe. Trish believed that I didn't want to have sex with her because I was a virgin, because that's what she wanted to believe. Gunnar believed I *had* had sex, because that's what he wanted to believe.

When Kimberly and Trish came back from the bathroom, Kimberly had a headache and wanted to go home. I knew this was yet another lie. Trish had told Kimberly everything, and now they wanted to go home and giggle about it. I could tell from the little mocking smirk on Kimberly's face.

We drove the girls home and did our non-orgy kissing thing where Gunnar and Kimberly kissed at the front porch, and Trish and I kissed at the car.

"You don't have anything to be ashamed of," Trish said, whispering again. "And don't worry, I won't tell anyone."

Her lie might have been more convincing if, back at the club, she'd waited at least two minutes before running off to tell Kimberly. But I was the practiced liar in this relationship, not Trish.

"Call me?" Trish said, prancing away.

"You bet!" I said with a confident wave.

Then Gunnar drove me home, and my second date with Trish Baskin was finally—finally!—over. I got out of the car and watched him drive away, even though it was still raining outside.

*Docious,* I thought. But I definitely meant "holy shit," not "hot damn."

Later that night, I stood by the stinky picnic gazebo staring up at the stars. The rain had finally stopped, and everything was now bright and clean and clear. The stars looked like they actually had little pointy things on them.

"Hey," a voice said.

I turned. It was Kevin. I'd IMed him thirty minutes earlier and told him that I'd really needed to see him, and to meet me here. Then I'd changed out of my wet clothes and come to wait for him.

"Hey," I said.

"'Sup?" His voice was soft and measured, like a surgeon talking to an anxious family in a hospital waiting room. He could tell something was wrong.

I opened my mouth and told him everything that had happened earlier that evening. I may have taken a breath, but I'm not sure.

When I finally stopped talking, Kevin hesitated a second longer, making sure I was finished. Then he said, "Man, that really sucks. Trish sounds like a real bitch."

"No," I said. "She just wanted what everyone wants. I just didn't want it with her." For some reason, I couldn't look at Kevin when I said this. Good thing there were the stars.

"Still," Kevin said. "She didn't have to say those things. She didn't have to say you were gay. It was like she was tryin' to scare you into doin' her."

I glanced at Kevin, but he was looking down at his shoes. "You must've turned a lot of girls down," I said.

He hunched his shoulders. "Not as many as I should've."

I wasn't jealous at the thought of Kevin having sex with girls. I figured it had to be about as exciting as my experience with Trish.

"Russel?" Kevin said. I wasn't looking at him now, but I could tell he wasn't looking at his shoes anymore, or the stars either. He was looking right at me. I thought, Why is there never a good fog when you need one?

"I should go!" I said. "I just really needed a friend to listen. Thanks for listening!"

Kevin didn't say anything. He just stood there, a stone guardian watching me as I started my march away.

I'd only made it a couple of feet when I realized

that I'd just said yet another lie in a whole evening of lies. If I'd really needed a "friend," I would have IMed Min. But it had been Kevin I'd wanted to see, and not to tell him what had happened with Trish.

I turned to face him, to tell him I was tired not just of lies, but of loneliness. Meeting the other members of the Geography Club, being open with them, had been important, but it had only been the preparation before the start of my journey. I'd learned about the places I wanted to go, I'd talked about them with my friends, but I hadn't actually set foot outside my door. The terrain of my own heart, the landscape of love, was still entirely unexplored. But people are right when they say the hardest step of every journey is the first, and I was scared. (Okay, I was terrified.)

"It's all right," Kevin said, softly, sensitively. "We don't have to do anything you don't want to do. And if we do anything at all, we'll be safe." So Kevin knew the truth. Why I'd contacted him tonight. What I really wanted from him. And it sounded like he wanted the same thing, like he was ready to leave on the very same voyage with me.

The funny thing was, suddenly I wasn't nervous anymore. I don't know if it was what Kevin had said, or if I was finally just sick and tired of feeling so alone—just like the night I'd agreed to meet Kevin, someone I didn't even know, at this stinky picnic gazebo in the first place.

In any event, I stepped up to Kevin and kissed him. In the close confines of his arms, it felt like I had stepped right up into the stars themselves—like I had become one with the sky, and that together we were as clean and pure and wide as the universe itself.

## CHAPTER NINE

I got to third base. At baseball practice the following Monday, that is. As for what happened that night with Kevin at the stinky picnic gazebo, that's none of your damn business.

But I suppose I should tell you anyway. If I was reading this and I didn't tell me what happened, I'd be pissed.

So here's what happened.

We were standing there kissing with that whole stars-and-universe thing going on. And it was nothing whatsoever like kissing Trish Baskin. For one thing, his breath was better. And unlike when Trish kissed me

126

and I didn't really kiss her back, Kevin was definitely kissing me back. (Boy, was he kissing me back!)

But it was just kissing, no groping or fumbling or even very much hugging. And since you can just kiss for only so long, eventually, we sort of pulled back and stood there facing each other.

"Man," Kevin said. "I've wanted to do that for so long."

It took me a second to catch my breath. Then I said, "What?"

"I wanted to kiss you. Ever since that first night when we met here? I wanted to kiss you then. Before that even. Why do you think I joined the Geography Club? I like everyone okay, but you're the reason I joined. To be with you."

I could hardly believe my ears. Kevin Land had joined the Geography Club to be with me? *He* wanted *me*? But I could see it on his face. Min had been right. Kevin Land wanted me.

I'm going to repeat this for emphasis, and because I really like the way it looks written down.

Kevin Land wanted me!

Kevin Land *wanted* me!

Kevin Land wanted *me*!

Sorry to go off like that, but learning that Kevin Land had a crush on me took me completely by surprise.

Of course, I knew how pathetic all this would sound if I said it out loud. So all I said was, "I wanted to kiss you too."

He stepped closer to me, and I felt his arms circle around me again and his hands rest on the small of my back. "I love your eyes," he said. "You have great eyes."

"How do you know?" I said. "It's too dark to see them." (Yes, I know this was totally the wrong thing to say. Give me a break—I was new at this.)

But Kevin just smiled. "I remember what they look like. It's like they're green and gray and brown and yellow, all at the same time." Just plain old hazel, I thought. (At least I knew enough not to say this.)

I felt one hand slide up the side of my body and touch my hair. "And your hair," Kevin said. "I've never seen hair this color before either. It's the color of autumn leaves." His hand moved to my face, gently feeling my cheeks, my nose, my lips, and my chin. "Best-lookin' guy in third period P.E., that's for sure."

"What about Jarred?" I said. Jarred Gasner was a guy in our P.E. class, and yes, I immediately regretted saying this too.

"You're much better-lookin' than Jarred," Kevin said. "He's kind of cute. But you're handsome."

"Am not."

Kevin smiled again, and his teeth glowed in the darkness. "You are."

"Can I ask you a question?" I said, desperate to change the subject—and at the same time, not wanting it ever to change.

"Sure," Kevin said.

"When did you know you were gay?"

He shrugged. "I guess I've always known. I just always liked being around guys. I like that they're bold and confident. That they're not afraid to take risks."

"Oh," I said, thinking, In other words, you like guys who are the complete opposite of me.

"Russel?" Kevin said.

"Huh?" I said.

"Can I kiss you again?"

I couldn't very well turn him down now—not after what he'd said about liking guys who took risks. Then again, I didn't *want* to turn him down. So I nodded, and he kissed me. His lips were firm and strong, his chin and face rough with whiskers.

We kept kissing, only this time there may have been some groping and fumbling and hugging. I think

I'll end this scene here, though. After all, a guy should be allowed to keep some secrets, shouldn't he?

I had my first baseball practice that Monday afternoon, and I didn't completely suck. Unfortunately, here "I didn't completely suck" doesn't mean "I was actually pretty good." It just means I didn't completely suck. But at one of my times up at bat, I really did manage to make it to third base.

Halfway through practice, Coach told the team to pair up, and before I could stop myself, I glanced over at Kevin. A couple of other guys looked like they were trying to catch Kevin's eye too, so I was flattered when he drifted over toward me.

Before I knew it, Coach had directed us out to the outfield, where the pairs of us were supposed to practice our throwing and catching. Kevin would slam the ball into my mitt (*thwap!*), and I'd do my best to heave it back at him (*thwumph*).

At first, it felt stilted and awkward. My aim was lousy, and even though Kevin was obviously going easy on me, his pitches still hit my mitt so hard, they stung my hand.

*Thwap!*
*Thwumph.*

*Thwap!*

*Thwumph.*

But then something strange happened. It was like we fell into some sort of groove. The ball kept whizzing back and forth, and it felt like we were connected somehow—like it was electricity zipping back and forth on a shiny copper wire. The ball itself was alive, and suddenly so were we—fresh and alert and raw.

*Thwap!*

*Thwumph.*

*Thwap!*

*Thwumph.*

Kevin would throw and I would catch, then I would throw and he would catch, and as we did, the other baseball players all around us in the outfield fell away. Now we were completely alone, like two simmering volcanoes side by side on some deserted tropical island in the middle of a calm blue sea.

*Thwap!*

*Thwumph.*

*Thwap!*

*Thwumph.*

I stared at Kevin, at the graceful flow of his perfectly proportioned body, at the shocks of his dark hair poking recklessly out from under his cap. I thought, Is playing baseball always like this? (I also thought, It's a good thing I'm wearing a cup!)

Ironically, only two hours before, I'd decided to quit the baseball team. My reasoning went like this: I'd joined the team to get closer to Kevin, but after Saturday night, I was now about as close to Kevin as I was going to get. Still, I'd planned to wait a few weeks to actually leave the team, until some semi-believable excuse presented itself. That way, Kevin wouldn't think I'd joined the team *only* because of him, which somehow still seemed too pathetic for words.

But now I was thinking, Hey, this baseball stuff isn't so bad! It sure beat my dates with Trish.

"Okay!" Coach called from home plate, and suddenly I was back in the outfield, with my awkward aim and stinging palm. "Let's try hitting a few more!"

On our way back to the dugout, Kevin said to me, "Dip?"

I had no idea what he was talking about. I was pretty sure he wasn't asking me to dance.

He must've seen the confusion on my face, because he flashed me his round tin of chewing tobacco. "Chew," he said. "You wanna chew?"

"Oh." Suddenly, I understood why I'd spent the

first part of the practice dodging wads of spit. It hadn't occurred to me that the team members were actually spitting *something*. Duh.

I'd never chewed tobacco before. (I'd only smoked cigarettes twice.) And the thing was, I didn't particularly *want* to chew tobacco. When it came to putting cancer-causing toxins into my body, I was no Gunnar, but I was a bit of a health nut. Then I remembered what Kevin had said about liking his guys bold and confident and willing to take risks. Besides, I was a baseball player now; I had to try chewing tobacco at least once, right?

"'Sokay," Kevin said to me, slipping the tin back into his pants. "You don't have to if you don't want to."

"No," I said. "I want to."

"Really," he said. "It's no big deal."

I waggled my eyebrows at him. "Hey, you should know by now that I like to try new things."

He laughed and blushed a little, then twisted open the tin for me to help myself.

I tried it, and sure enough, I didn't like it. It tasted like shredded leather marinated in warm vinegar. But I kept it in anyway, mostly because I didn't want to disappoint Kevin. Meanwhile, I was thinking, So what if

I'm making one tiny little compromise for Kevin's sake? Wasn't compromise part of what relationships were supposed to be all about?

On Tuesday, the day after my first baseball practice, the Geography Club met again.

"Well?" Terese demanded. "Where is she?" She was talking to Min and Kevin and Ike and me, and she was talking *about* Belinda Sherman. True to her word, Belinda had come to our meeting last Thursday. Since no one wanted her there, and since no one sure as hell wanted to talk about geography, it had been one very awkward meeting. After about ten minutes, we'd ended the meeting with some vague talk about getting back into geography the following week.

This week.

Today.

"Maybe she quit," Kevin said hopefully. That had been the unofficial plan on Thursday. Be so boring and disorganized that she'd want nothing to do with us.

But Min said, "No such luck. I ran into her today. She said she was bringing in some geography board game this afternoon. God knows why, but I think she's here to stay."

We stood there for a second, all of us sending out

waves of psychic discouragement to Belinda, wherever the hell in the school she was at that exact moment. Ike looked particularly annoyed, but then I noticed that whenever he glanced at me, his scowl seemed to deepen. That's when I knew it wasn't just Belinda Sherman he was irritated with. I'd been right about Ike being hot for Kevin, and now he was jealous of what was going on between Kevin and me. I hadn't told him what had happened on Saturday night—I'd only told Min, who'd been very excited for me and who'd managed to restrain herself enough to say "I told you so" only one single time. But Min had to have told Terese about Kevin and me, and she'd probably told Ike.

"Well," Terese said to the group. "That's it then. If Belinda shows, that's the end of the Geography Club. What's the point?"

"No!" I said. I hadn't meant to speak so loudly, but I was passionate. I didn't want the Geography Club to end—which I guess meant I hadn't joined the Geography Club just to get together with Kevin after all. Or if I had, the club had since become important to me for other reasons. Because I had Kevin now, but I still desperately wanted the Geography Club to go on.

I glanced at the door to Kephart's classroom,

which was still closed. Belinda was nowhere to be seen.

"There has to be something we can do," I said.

"We could always start another club," Ike said.

Min shook her head. "Belinda would know. She works in the office, remember? She'll see our names on the application."

"So what?" Terese said. "So what if we hurt her feelings?"

"It's not that," Min said. "She could report us, say we deliberately excluded her, maybe even say it's because she's black. It'd just call attention to our club, and that's the last thing we need."

I thought about this, but no matter how I turned it over in my head, there didn't seem to be any way out.

"God *damn* it!" Terese said. "I was really starting to like this damn club."

"Yeah, me too," Ike said, taking a break from glowering at me.

"It's not fair!" I said, and everyone looked at me. "Why can't there be just one place for gay kids, where we don't have to hide who we are? Hell, straight people have the whole rest of the world! They go around holding hands and kissing and talking about 'my-girlfriend-this' and 'my-boyfriend-that.' And they say *we* shove our lifestyle in *their* faces? That's a laugh!"

I was pretty riled up. But I wasn't so excited that I couldn't sense a change in the air. We all turned toward the classroom doorway, which, of course, Belinda Sherman was now standing in, with a large orange shoulder bag at her side. How the hell she had opened the door without anyone hearing, I don't know. But she had. And even if she hadn't heard absolutely everything we'd said, she'd heard enough. You could see it in her eyes.

We stared at her and she stared at us. She knew. And everyone there, including Belinda, also knew that she could ruin us all.

Min was the one who finally broke the silence. "Are you going to tell?" she said softly.

Belinda stood there thinking for what seemed like a minute or more, but was probably only ten seconds. Then she closed the door behind her and faced us, so there were now six of us alone in that classroom.

"My mom's an alcoholic," she said at last.

I thought, What the hell does that have to do with anything? If Belinda Sherman was quirky like Gunnar, always saying the wrong thing at the wrong time, I sure as hell didn't want to hear it right then. I and every other member of the Geography Club wanted to know one thing, and one thing only: was she going to tell the rest of the school about us?

"She's always drunk," Belinda went on. "My mom. She doesn't get really, really drunk that often, but when she does, she tells everyone she's sick. I think sometimes she even believes it. I guess because sometimes she *is* sick, and I always have to clean it up."

"That's interesting," Terese said to her. "But it doesn't answer the question. Are you going to tell on us or not?"

"No, wait," Min said. "Let her talk." I wanted Belinda to go on talking too. I had an idea where she was going with this. Besides, pissing off Belinda Sherman didn't strike me as a real good plan just then.

"People are always talking about their families," Belinda said. "How they all went out to Chuck E. Cheese for pizza, or how they just got back from their latest trip to Disneyland. The whole world has to tell me over and over again how normal they are, and how different they are from me. And I have to just sit there and listen, because no one wants to hear the truth, that my family has never been to Disneyland and never will go." Belinda looked directly at me. "So I know what you mean when you talk about people always shoving something in your face. And I know what it's like to have to hide."

I'd been right. Belinda wasn't being quirky like Gunnar. She was answering Min's question. She was just going about it in a roundabout way.

I stared at Belinda. She had seemed bright and bubbly before, but she didn't now. The loud clothes and the smiley-face earrings? They were just part of an act she put on. In other words, Belinda had something else in common with the rest of us. She was a good liar.

Now Belinda looked directly at Min. "Don't worry," she said. "I won't tell anyone about your club. And I'll leave you alone. I won't be comin' back." She turned for the door.

"Wait," I said, and she stopped.

I glanced at the others, and we held a conversation with our eyes. The Geography Club wasn't really about being gay, we all seemed to agree. It was ultimately about something else, some sense of being an outsider, a vagabond, with no place to call home. Whatever it was about, Belinda obviously qualified as a member.

"You want to stay?" I said to Belinda.

Belinda looked confused. "But I'm straight."

"We're an after-school club," Kevin said. "We're

not supposed to discriminate."

Belinda cocked her head. "You really don't care?"

"Well," Min said, "don't expect us to spend much time talking about geography."

Belinda giggled. "Damn! I'm a token straight!" Her laughter, which had been so annoying the week before, now had a musical ring to it. It was contagious too, because the rest of us joined in.

And that was how the all-gay Geography Club got its first straight member.

That Friday, I had my first baseball game. Coach put me in left field, which, if you know anything about baseball, isn't exactly where they put the star player. But I was new, and I didn't want the responsibility of a more important position anyway (unlike Kevin, who played first base). Way out in left field, there was only so much damage I could do, which may not have been the attitude of a winner, but it was my attitude in baseball, so there you go. Still, I did manage to catch a couple of fly balls, even if I fumbled a couple too.

My first time up at bat, I was just praying I wouldn't strike out. I did manage to hit the damn ball, and even made it to second base before our next batter hit a pop fly, and that ended our time at bat.

In high school baseball, you only play seven innings, and by the time we reached the top of the last one, I was actually kind of having fun. It was now officially spring, and the sun was officially shining, and I'd decided that baseball wasn't nearly as boring when you're playing it as when you're watching it. Best of all, I hadn't made a complete fool out of myself all game long. (The secret to happiness in life: low expectations.)

By the bottom of the seventh inning, we were behind six to eight when it came my turn to bat. This was exactly the kind of pressure I didn't want. We only had one out, so my striking out now wouldn't technically lose us the game. But it wouldn't win me any new friends either.

"Come on, Russel!" Kevin shouted as I grabbed a bat and helmet and did my best saunter up to the plate. "Outta the park!" Coach and the other guys on the team probably yelled out encouraging things too, but I wasn't really listening to them.

I took a couple of practice swings and stared out at the pitcher. He looked clean-cut and wholesome, but there was determination in his eyes, like he had dedicated himself to the principles of hot dogs, apple pie, and striking me out. Still, Kevin had told me that baseball was as much a psychological game as a physical one, and that intimidating the pitcher with a confident stare was an important part of playing.

The first pitch was way wide, but like an idiot, I swung anyway, and like a clumsy idiot, I even stumbled a little. My stare may have been intimidating, but my depth perception just plain sucked.

"Eye on the ball!" Kevin called. "Eye on the ball!"

The next pitch was wide too. I was all set to swing again, but at the last second, I pulled back, and I heard the umpire shout "Ball!" When I looked back at the pitcher's eyes, I could suddenly see that these wide pitches were no accident. He saw that I was green, and he was trying to lure me into hitting bad balls. But now I saw through him. I knew what he was up to. Of course, he saw through me too, and he knew that I knew, which meant the end of the bad balls. But there was really something to this staring-the-pitcher-in-the-eye thing.

"Atta boy!" Kevin called. "Good eye, good eye!"

I scanned the bases. We had a guy on first and a guy on third. If I struck out, I'd be helping to cost us the game. But if I hit a home run, well, two guys plus me equals three, and that would actually win the game.

And if elephants laid eggs, it'd take sixteen people

to eat a three-egg omelette.

I stepped up to the plate again, waited for the pitcher's windup, and then promptly got my second strike. More proof of the power of negative thinking.

"'Sokay!" Kevin said encouragingly. "It only takes one hit!"

Okay, I thought. No more negative thoughts. This was too important. It was one of those defining, do-or-die moments in life. Not just do-or-die for the game. It was do-or-die for Kevin and me too. If I struck out now, I'd be too embarrassed to ever show my face around him again.

The pitcher threw the ball.

I swung.

And what do you know? My bat connected with the baseball exactly the way that eraser had connected with that Ping-Pong ball back when the Geography Club had been playing classroom baseball. There was a very clean, very satisfying *crack!* and the ball soared up, up, up, and out—as in out of the ballpark.

Yes, I actually hit a home run. I also won us the game. The crowd didn't exactly roar—there were only fifty or so spectators, and only about thirty-five of them were rooting for the home team. But thirty-five people can make quite a bit of noise, especially when they're shouting and clapping and carrying on like ten-year-olds at an after-school birthday party.

For a second, I just stood there gaping, like this was all some kind of mistake. (There was nothing I could do that was so great that I couldn't somehow make it look stupid.)

But then I heard Kevin's voice cut through the din. "Go!" he said. "Run the bases!"

So I ran the bases—it was really more of a jog. I went from first to second to third before finally heading for home, where the whole team was jumping up and down and shouting, and where Kevin was waiting for me with his patented grin, ready to pound me on the back. People cheered me all the while. I'd never been cheered for anything before, and it felt good. (Okay, it felt great!)

None of this seemed like it was happening in slow motion, but you can imagine it that way if you want. It makes a much better picture that way. I wish it *had* been in slow motion, though. I could have enjoyed the glory a little longer. And it would have been that much longer before all the horrible things that happened in the days that followed.

## CHAPTER TEN

*"Middlebroooooook!"* Ramone said to me in the locker room after the game. "Way to *smack* it!"

The baseball team was supposedly getting undressed so we could all shower and go home. But what everyone was really doing was whooping it up and telling me how great I was for winning the game. So far, the other guys on the team had patted, slapped, prodded, and hoisted me—pretty much everything one guy could do to another guy in a public place and not get arrested.

"That was *excellent*, Middlebrook!" Nate said. "Right over those dickheads!"

I felt like the winner of a beauty pageant, with all

the other contestants gathering around me and showering me with bouquets at the end of the competition. (This probably isn't the butchest comparison, but it was the way I felt, so what can you do?)

"How'd you hit it like that?" Jarred asked me. "Huh, Middlebrook?"

"Shoot, that was easy," I said. "I just pretended the ball was the pitcher's head!" I was no fool. I knew what sort of material would work on a crowd like this.

Sure enough, Jarred and everyone else laughed. I was laughing now too, and it was at that exact moment that something incredible occurred to me.

I was actually enjoying myself.

Enjoying myself? I had never *enjoyed* myself in the boys' locker room before! Always before, it had felt like I was a spy in hostile territory, and it was only a matter of time until I was exposed (see chapter one, section one). But now here I was, laughing and joking with the best of them. Sure, it was a little distracting that half the guys were naked or waltzing around in just their jockstraps. I also knew most of these guys were boneheads who couldn't talk their way out of a paper bag.

But at the same time, I felt this strange sense of camaraderie. It was as if I'd never even been in this locker room before. As if all my life, I'd been dressing and undressing in the cold hallway outside, only overhearing little bits of the conversation. But now my membership had been accepted, and I'd been welcomed inside. Plus, there was full-frontal male nudity.

I looked at Kevin, undressing over by our lockers. He winked at me. Then he grabbed a towel and turned for the showers, his dimpled ass flexing as he went. He was the only guy on the team who hadn't hugged me since the game had ended. I didn't mind. We'd make up for it later.

The next day, Saturday, I met Gunnar for a game of racquetball. In the YMCA locker room, I told him about my victory in the baseball game.

"That's fantastic!" he said to me. "I had no idea you were such a great baseball player! But I guess I should've known, right? I mean, you always beat me in racquetball, don't you? And bowling—you beat me in that too. And croquet! No, wait, sometimes I beat you in croquet. That and putt-putt. Or do you beat me in putt-putt? I just wish I could've come to your game. I'll come to the next game, okay? Is that all right? Can I come to the next game? Wow, I still can't believe you won the game like that; that's so fantastic!"

Gunnar was very happy for me. Too happy. Something was up.

"What?" I said to him.

"What what?" he said innocently. He said this a lot lately, and it was starting to piss me off.

"You want something from me. You want me to go out with Trish again, don't you?"

"Why?" Gunnar said, just a little too quickly. "Do you *want* to go out with her? Because I think I might be able to arrange that. I mean, I could call Kimberly and see what she says, but I'm not making any promises." I rolled my eyes. Gunnar trying to not sound eager about my going out with Trish came across even phonier than his being so incredibly excited about my winning the baseball game.

So Trish wanted to go out with me yet again. And that meant she thought when I'd said I didn't want to have sex with her, I'd only meant I didn't want to have sex with her *yet*.

"No," I said to Gunnar, as firmly as I could to someone who wasn't a child. "I don't want to go out with Trish again."

"Really? Because I thought we had a pretty good—"

"No!" I looked Gunnar straight in the eye. "I

really don't want to go out with Trish."

"But Kimberly—"

"Look!" I said. "The answer is no!"

We finished dressing for our game in a frigid silence. Then we walked to the racquetball court in that same cold hush.

Once inside the court, Gunnar turned to me and said, "It's not like I ask you for that many favors."

"You asked me to go out with Trish twice before, and both times I went. But I'm not doing it a third time."

Gunnar's big blue eyes stared at me. "Russ, please." His voice began to quiver, and for a second, I thought he was going to cry. "I'll owe you one. A big one. I'll do anything you want." I did want to help him—who wants to see a friend in pain? But a third date with Trish Baskin was nonnegotiable, especially since I was starting to think she might have decided a third date would qualify as the "special" time I was waiting for before I had sex.

"Why don't you just go out with Kimberly alone?" I said. "Why do you always want Trish and me to come along?" I already knew the answer to this question— Kimberly didn't *want* to go out with Gunnar alone. But I figured if I could get him to finally see this, maybe he wouldn't want to go out with Kimberly either.

In frustration, Gunnar swung his racquet through the air (dangerously close to my head, I might add). "I don't *know*!" he said. "Kimberly always just says she wants to double with you and Trish. Maybe she's just shy."

I thought, Kimberly *shy*? How could someone as smart as Gunnar possibly believe this?

It was time to be blunt. The truth hurt, but it was also supposed to set you free.

"Look," I said. "I don't think Kimberly treats you all that good. I think she's just going out with you because Trish wants to go out with me."

Gunnar looked up at me with hatred in his eyes. *"That's not true!"* The shrillness of his voice echoed down at me from the high ceiling of the court.

"Okay!" I said quickly. I admit I was taken aback. "Okay, it was just an idea."

"Well, it was a *stupid* one!"

It had been a stupid idea, but not for the reason Gunnar thought. It was stupid, because there was no way someone who wanted a girlfriend as badly as Gunnar did was going to give up so easily, even on someone as thoroughly unattractive as Kimberly Peterson.

"Let's just play," I said. "Okay?"

Without another word, he snatched the ball and started hammering away at it. His first five serves were so fast I couldn't return any of them. When I finally won the serve, he won it right back again. This wasn't the Gunnar I knew. I'd never seen him be so single-minded about anything in his life.

Toward the end of the game, he whirled on me at last. "Why don't you want to go out with Trish anyway?"

"What?" I said.

"What's the problem? Don't you think she's nice?"

"She's okay."

"Don't you think she's good-looking?"

"No, she's okay."

"Then what? What's the real reason?" The boldness still hadn't left his eyes.

I didn't have an answer, at least not one for him.

"It's just not there," I said at last. "I don't feel anything for her."

"For her, huh? That's funny. 'Cause I don't remember you feeling anything for anyone else either."

I really didn't like where this conversation was heading. All I could think to say was "What?"

"What *what*?" Gunnar said. "I'm just saying I can't remember you ever being interested in *any* girl."

Suddenly, I was sweating, but not from the racquetball. This was the cold, clammy sweat of fear. Exactly what was Gunnar saying? What did he know, and how long had he known it?

"Did Trish say something?" I said. It *was* Trish—it had to be! But if she was telling people I was gay, why would she want to go out with me again?

"Like what?" Gunnar said innocently—too innocently. "It just seems funny. I mean, a big baseball star like you, but you don't have a girlfriend? Don't you think that's funny? I think people might think that's funny."

"Okay!" I shouted, and it echoed too, just as shrilly as Gunnar's voice had a minute before.

"'Okay,' what?" Gunnar said.

I lowered my voice. "I'll go out with Trish again. Okay? That's what you want, right? I'll go out with her. Anytime you say. Let's just finish the game, okay?"

Gunnar walked back to the serve line, and we did finish that game. I hope it goes without saying that he whipped my ass.

• • •

The following Monday, the whole school knew I had won the baseball game. I wasn't sure *how* everyone knew—there had only been thirty-five people at the game. True, there was an article about it in the *Goodkind Gazette*, but the whole school was back to not reading the school newspaper, so I knew no one had found out about me there. But somehow word had got out. Now people I had never spoken to before, people who I didn't even think knew who I was, called out my name in the hallways. Two times during the day, groups of people actually fell silent as I walked by. (It is impossible not to feel incredibly flattered by this.) Even some teachers, who you'd expect to be above this kind of thing, had a little glint in their eyes when they talked to me. And when I ended up being fifty cents short for my food in the cafeteria lunch line, the cashier just winked at me and sent me on my way.

A week earlier, I might've been freaked out by all this attention, but I'd already become an old hand at the fame game, so I took it all in stride.

But that afternoon after baseball practice, I realized I'd left a book back in my locker. So before heading for my bike, I veered back to the main building.

The front doors to the school weren't locked yet, but the halls were long since empty, and most of the lights had been turned off. The concrete floors, which had already been mopped, smelled of ammonia and dirt.

I started down the hallway and heard voices coming from around the corner. Ordinarily, hearing voices in the deserted hallways after school might have made me uneasy—especially loud, obnoxious, male voices. I might even have gone a roundabout way just to avoid running into whoever it was. But these days, I owned this school. For the first time in my life, I didn't have anything to be afraid of.

I rounded that corner and found myself face-to-face with Jarred and Nolan, two guys from the baseball team. Coach had kept me and a few other guys a little later at practice to help us with our hitting, so everyone else had got out early. Now Jarred and Nolan were standing at the base of the stairway to the second floor, which was exactly where I needed to go.

"Yo, Middlebrook!" Nolan said. "'Sup?"

"Hey," I said. "Forgot a book." Knowing these guys were both on the baseball team, I felt myself relax a little. I guess I hadn't been quite as comfortable rounding that corner as I'd thought.

"Hey," Jarred said, "you go out with Trish Baskin, right?"

"What?" I said. "Oh yeah." I *did* go out with Trish Baskin, even if it was against my will. But so much for my feeling relaxed.

"She's pretty hot," Jarred said, and I wasn't sure about the protocol here. Should I say thanks or what?

"What 'bout her friend Kimberly?" Nolan said, more to Jarred than to me. Then he laughed and made the Hannibal Lecter lip-smacking sound from that movie *The Silence of the Lambs.*

"Yeah," I said, and I hope I don't need to tell you what I was thinking here. "Well," I added, "later."

I stepped between Jarred and Nolan and put a foot on the bottom stair, and everything would've been just fine if, just then, Brian Bund hadn't suddenly appeared in the bend in the stairway above me. My first thought was, What the hell is Brian doing here at school this long after classes? But he had a stack of books in his arms—of course, he was carrying them like a girl—so I decided he must have been coming from the library, which would have just closed for the afternoon.

My second thought was, Please don't let Jarred

and Nolan see him! It was just dark enough that if they didn't look up, they might not notice he was there, especially if Brian was smart enough not to move.

But then Jarred looked at me and glanced up at where I was looking.

"Brian!" he said with exaggerated enthusiasm. "How ya *doin'*?" Now it was too late. Brian had been spotted.

Brian didn't move a muscle.

"What's wrong?" Nolan said, with fake innocence. "Don't you wanna come down?"

Brian thought for a second, considering his options. The only other stairway from the second floor was on the other side of the building. And he had to know that turning around and running now might do him more harm than good.

"Come on," Nolan coaxed. "We won't hurt you."

Brian hesitated a second longer, then tentatively stepped down the stairs until he was just a couple of feet above us. But of course, the closer Brian got to the bottom, the taller Jarred and Nolan stood, and the more they moved to the middle of the steps. It didn't help that I was standing between them, so the three of us were effectively blocking his exit.

"Would you look at him?" Nolan said to Jarred,

both of them laughing. "How scared he looks?" Brian *did* look scared. Now that he'd moved into the light, we could see the wide-eyed, flushed expression on his face, but to me, it was anything but funny.

Brian Bund had always been treated like crap at our school. But ever since Ms. Toles had given that stupid interview to the school newspaper, everyone really had decided that he was the gay kid she was talking about. Since then, people had been treating Brian even worse. At first, I'd assumed all this extra teasing would eventually fade, like an overplayed pop song. But everyone had turned this song into the school anthem, and now they played it every chance they got. If I'd been Brian, I would have looked wary too.

"He looks like he's seeing a damn ghost!" Nolan said.

"Or a monster!" Jarred said. "He looks like he's seeing a monster!"

I thought, Good quip, Jarred—seeing a monster is *totally* different from seeing a ghost. (Jarred wasn't the brightest star in the nebula, but he sure looked good in his underpants.)

Nolan glanced at me. "Hey, Middlebrook, what do you think he looks like?"

So here I was. Suddenly, I'd found myself in

another one of those defining, do-or-die moments. It was just like the Friday before, when I'd been up at bat in the bottom of the seventh. There weren't any crowds watching me this time, just Nolan and Jarred. But I felt a lot more pressure from the two of them than I had from the crowd and the team the Friday before. It felt more important too. This wasn't just about some stupid baseball game. It was about someone else's feelings.

I'd like to say I rose to the occasion, just like I had on Friday. That I walked confidently up to the plate of that high school hallway and told Jarred and Nolan to go fuck themselves.

But I can't say I did that, because this time, I stepped up to the plate, swung, and missed the ball completely.

I said to Jarred and Nolan, "He looks like a mouse trapped in the coils of a python. Look at his face—you can almost see his whiskers quivering."

Jarred and Nolan both had to think about this for a second, working through it in their minds. It was more complicated than their usual jeers. But finally Nolan laughed, and then Jarred did too.

"Hey, Middlebrook!" Nolan said. "That's pretty good!"

I laughed too, but I felt the exact opposite of happy. I'd never teased Brian before for anything. I'd never even laughed at him.

I was a shit, okay? I knew it then too. All I can say is what Kevin and I had been doing in the dark at the stinky picnic gazebo wasn't the only traveling I'd been doing lately. I'd also been traveling to a place called the Land of the Popular, and the view from there was pretty damn good. When you threw in my new friends in the Geography Club and my dating Kevin Land—*Kevin Land!*—well, the Land of the Popular was pretty much paradise. I'd only been in paradise for two days, and I sure as hell wasn't ready to go back home just yet. (At least we weren't ridiculing Brian for being gay. I definitely wouldn't have joined in if they'd been ridiculing him for being gay. At least that's what I told myself.)

We kept laughing at Brian, and Nolan said, "Boo!" and Brian actually flinched, God damn him.

Jarred growled like a monster, but at least this time, Brian didn't flinch.

I couldn't think of a sound to make that sounded like a python, so I growled like a monster too.

Through it all, we all laughed except Brian.

And then, just when I thought I couldn't feel any

more miserable, I looked back at Brian and saw that Min had stepped onto the landing above him. She had books in her arms too, like she'd also come from the library.

Even as I was still laughing at Brian, my eyes met Min's. It was like when I'd been trying to stare down the pitcher in that baseball game the week before. But there was no way I was going to stare Min down. Because I could see in her eyes that she had seen and heard everything that I had just said and done.

## CHAPTER ELEVEN

Min didn't talk to me in that hallway after school, when Nolan and Jarred and I had been laughing at Brian Bund. She just watched me for a second more, then without saying a word, marched down the stairs, pushing her way between Nolan and me. I quickly stepped out of her way. Brian, smart guy that he was, took the opportunity to hightail it out of there in her wake.

"What's *her* problem?" Nolan said. Min was pretty obviously pissed.

"Bitch," Jarred said. But I noticed that both of them had finally stopped laughing.

I didn't talk to Min later that night either. She

didn't IM me, and I didn't IM her. And the next day, she ate lunch not with Gunnar and me, but with some of her friends from the Girl Scouts.

Min didn't talk to me about what happened in that hallway with Brian, but somehow I had a feeling that this wasn't going to be the last I'd hear about it.

The next afternoon, at the Tuesday meeting of the Geography Club, Min walked into Kephart's classroom and said, "We have a problem." We almost never did the whole five-minute thing anymore, where we each had five minutes to say whatever we wanted. Now it was usually more of a free-flowing conversation.

"What kind of problem?" Belinda said. Min had been the last to arrive. Everyone else was already there.

"Brian Bund," Min said. Here we go, I thought. Now Min was going to tell everyone what I had done to Brian. She was obviously trying to punish me. I was kicking myself for not telling everyone my side of the story first. Then again, I wasn't exactly sure what I could have said.

"What about him?" Kevin said.

"People are really ripping into him," Min said. "It's terrible." She looked directly at me. "Isn't it, Russel?"

I didn't say anything, just looked down at the floor. What could I say? I deserved all the crap Min was flipping me, and more.

"It sucks," Terese said. "But you said 'we' have a problem. What does Brian have to do with us?"

"I just think we should do something."

"What?" Kevin said. "Why?"

"Come on," Min said. "Don't you guys feel bad for him? What must that be like?"

"Sure," Ike said. "Must be horrible. But what can we do?"

"For one thing," Min said, "we could invite him to join the Geography Club."

As soon as she said this, it got so quiet you could hear a pin drop. I thought, Why is she doing this to me? I told myself that this was just about her being competitive with me—that she was jealous of my newfound popularity, and she wanted to take me down a peg.

"Are you serious?" Terese said at last.

"Sure," Min said. "Why not?"

Kevin said, "Well, for one thing, we don't even know he's gay. That's what everyone says, but we don't know it's true. It probably ain't."

"That shouldn't matter," Min said. "Belinda's not gay."

"Yeah!" Belinda said directly to Kevin. "Watch it, buster."

"Besides," Min said, "everyone *thinks* he's gay. They rip into him *because* they think he's gay. And we're a support group for gay kids and kids who can relate to us. Don't we have some responsibility here?"

"No," Terese said. "We're a support group for us. What's happening to Brian is shitty, but it's not our job to make it better."

What *was* the purpose of the Geography Club? On that first day in Kephart's classroom, we'd talked about a lot of things, but we'd never really talked about that. It hadn't seemed important at the time, but now I saw that it kind of was.

But the fact was, we *were* a gay club. And Brian was being teased because people thought he was gay. Min was right. If we stood for anything at all, we did have a responsibility here. That's when I knew that this idea of Min's—inviting Brian to join us—wasn't about Min being competitive with me, or her trying to punish me. It was about her wanting to do the right thing.

"I don't know," Kevin said. "What if Brian talks? What if we tell him about the club, and he decides not to join, but then he tells someone about us?"

"He won't talk," Min said. "Are you kidding?

More than anyone, he knows what it's like to be an outcast. You really think he'd want to pass that on to us?"

"He might," Ike said. "You know what they say about drowning rats. That they can claw each other's eyes out."

"Come on," Min said. "These are just excuses. They're not the real reason you guys don't want him to join."

"Yeah?" Terese said. "Then what is?"

"Because it's Brian Bund," Min said.

No one said anything, which I guess proved her point.

"It's not just that," Terese said. "There's the whole gay thing. Everyone thinks Brian's gay. If he joins the Geography Club, they'll think we're gay too."

"Oh, that's just stupid!" Min said, and Terese stiffened a little. "We're the Geography Club. If anyone even asks—which no one will—we tell them Brian joined because he wanted to learn about geography. Who wouldn't believe that? No one's going to think anything at all."

When no one responded, Min said, "I think we should vote on it."

"Vote?" Belinda said, and Min explained how we'd decided at that first meeting that any conflicts be decided by a vote.

"That makes sense," Belinda said. "Well, I vote that we ask him to join. Build up the nongay contingent a bit."

"So do I," Min said firmly.

"Well, I'm against it," Terese said, and Min stared at her like Terese had just slapped her in the face. I wasn't sure why Min was so shocked. It had been clear from the way Terese was talking that she was going to vote against Brian. But I think Min had never considered that Terese would actually vote against her.

"Ike?" Belinda said.

"I don't know," he said. "I guess I think it's a bad idea."

"Me too," Kevin said. "I'm against it."

"What?" I said to Kevin. I was so surprised by what he'd said that I'd spoken aloud for the first time since Min had entered the room. Kevin was voting against asking Brian to join the Geography Club? It was so obviously the right thing to do! How could he not see that?

"It's too risky," Kevin said. "We're taking a big enough risk just meeting like this. The fewer people who know, the better."

"Russel?" Min said.

"Huh?" I said, still shocked by what Kevin had said. I'd been certain he was going to vote for Brian, which I guess was just as stupid as Min thinking Terese was going to vote for Brian. Instead, Kevin had voted against taking even a little tiny gamble in order to help Brian out. (So had Ike. So much for what Kevin said about guys being the ones who liked to take risks, I thought. I guess he just meant snowboarding or whatever.)

"How do you vote?" Min said to me.

"Me?" I said. I had been going to vote with Min. But now that I knew how Kevin had voted, I didn't know what to do. I didn't want to vote against him.

"What difference does it make how he votes?" Terese said suddenly. "The vote's two to three. Even if he votes for Brian, it'll just be three to three. In a tie vote, you stay with the status quo." She looked at Ike. "Isn't that right?"

He nodded. "Yeah. That's the way it works. You need a majority to do anything extra."

I breathed a sigh of relief. I was off the hook. I didn't have to decide between Kevin and Min.

"The rest of us voted," Min said. "Russel should

too." I instantly wanted to strangle her. Now she *was* trying to punish me! This *was* about her being competitive!

"But Terese's right!" I protested. "My vote won't make any difference."

"Still," Min said, looking directly at me. "It's only fair."

"Come *on*!" Terese said impatiently. "Just vote so we can get this over, and we can move on to something else."

Everyone was looking at me. Thanks to Min, I had to say something—but what? On one hand, I knew she was right about Brian; we *did* have a responsibility— and I especially had a responsibility to help him, to make up for what I'd done to him in the hallway with Jarred and Nolan. But Ike was right too, about my vote not counting anyway. It was just symbolic or whatever. It would have been different if my vote had actually mattered. There was no reason to risk making Kevin mad over a stupid symbolic vote. (But even as I thought this, I suddenly remembered what Ike had said about those drowning rats.)

"No," I said.

"'No,' what?" Min said.

Did she really need me to spell it out? "No," I said.

"I don't want Brian to join the Geography Club." The minute I said this, I thought, Why the hell didn't I abstain? Wasn't that always an option when you voted?

Now that I'd voted, I thought I saw Kevin relax a little—or was I imagining things? I couldn't look Min in the eye, but I didn't need to look at her to know that she was hating me with all her guts right then.

"Two to four," Terese said. "The motion fails." She was right, but she didn't have to sound so gleeful about it.

"Min?" Belinda said. "That okay with you?"

Min just gave a tight little nod. At least she wasn't looking at me anymore. I wondered if she'd ever look at me again.

I didn't think my week could get much worse. But then came Friday and my next date with Trish Baskin.

As usual, Gunnar drove, and once again, we picked up the girls on the corner at the end of Kimberly's street. We went for pizza at the very same pizza parlor where the Geography Club had met for the first time, but the meal couldn't have been more different. For one thing, Trish and Kimberly and Gunnar had no problem deciding on a pizza (pepperoni—no one even asked me what I wanted).

The conversation was different too. At one point during the meal, Kimberly said, "Mr. Donaldson is so hot! I would so fuck him if he wanted." Mr. Donaldson was one of our school's science teachers, and given that Kimberly's date, Gunnar, was sitting right next to her, her comment had to be something of a new low in tackiness. (Even without Gunnar sitting there, it was pretty tasteless.) But once again, my friend the doormat didn't seem to mind.

Later, as we were driving away from dinner, Kimberly turned around from the front seat of the car and said to Trish, "You sure you got the key?"

Trish nodded. "It's in my purse."

"Key?" I said.

"To my parents' beach place," Trish said.

"I thought we were going to a movie."

"Oh yeah," said Gunnar from the front seat. "I forgot to tell you. Trish snuck the key to her parents' beach place. We thought we could head out there instead of a movie."

"What's out at the beach place?" I said, but I already knew. There were bedrooms out at the beach place. Gunnar knew it too. That's why he'd lied and told me we were going to a movie. He knew I wouldn't have agreed to come otherwise.

Up in the front seat, Kimberly nestled up against Gunnar. Was she really going to have sex with him, someone she didn't even like, just because he managed to get me hooked up with Trish for one more night?

But that wasn't my problem. My problem was that one of those bedrooms out at the beach place was meant for Trish and me.

As much as I wanted to, I couldn't very well jump out of a moving car. And I couldn't demand that Gunnar pull over and let me out—not without embarrassing myself and Gunnar in the process. So before I knew it, Gunnar had parked the car in the gravel driveway of a darkened little cabin out along the water.

"Fucking *brrrr*!" Kimberly said once we were inside. "Turn on some heat!" The cabin was decorated in a kitschy nautical theme—lots of shells and seagulls and lighthouses and glass fishing floats.

"Russel?" Trish said. "You wanna build a fire?"

"I guess," I said.

As I was wadding up newspaper by the fireplace, I leaned over to Gunnar and said, "Why didn't you tell me we were coming out here?"

"I thought I did," he said. "I guess I forgot."

Even now, he couldn't tell me the truth. That annoyed me almost more than the original lie.

By the time the fire was burning, I turned to see that Kimberly was lighting a fire of her own: she'd found Trish's parents' liquor and was lining the bottles up on the seaman's chest that served as a coffee table.

"*Here* we go!" Kimberly said, marveling at all the alcoholic selections. At first, I thought she was going to insist that we all get bombed with her, which only proved that I still didn't know Kimberly Peterson very well. No, apparently the alcohol was only so she could get loaded *herself*. Once she started pounding them down, it was clear she couldn't have cared less about the rest of us.

"Just make sure you leave at least half in every bottle," Trish said, and Kimberly completely ignored her. If Trish really cared whether the bottles were still half full at the end of the evening, she needed to get herself a new best friend.

For the next hour or so, we sat around talking, and Kimberly got drunker and drunker, laughing at anything even remotely funny, and then laughing at things that weren't at all funny. I drank Coke, but Gunnar and Trish both followed Kimberly's lead and started tossing back shots. At the end of that hour, there was a lot less than half the alcohol left in each of the bottles lined up on that seaman's chest.

Gunnar got up to pee, and I pulled him aside. "Hey," I said. "You think maybe you had enough?"

"Huh?" He obviously wasn't thinking, or seeing, too clearly.

"You have to drive us home, remember?" Already I was thinking that I'd be the one driving us back, but I wanted to at least plant the idea that maybe we could be heading home before too long.

"I'm *fine*," he said, and he actually slurred the word. "'Sides, I was thinking we could spend the night out here!"

I didn't bother trying to argue. I knew there was nothing I could say to change his mind. He was like the sea captain in one of the wave-tossed ships in the tacky ocean paintings on the walls of this cabin; despite the obvious storm warnings, he was determined to see this voyage through.

When Gunnar and I returned to the party, Gunnar cuddled up next to Kimberly, and Trish cuddled up next to me. Then Kimberly said, "Hey! Let's play a game!" I had an idea she wasn't talking about pinochle, so I wasn't very surprised when she then announced, "Let's play Truth or Dare!"

That perked Trish up. "Good idea!"

"I'm gonna go first!" Kimberly said. She turned to Gunnar and said seductively, "Truth or dare!"

"Dare," he said, and at least he had the decency to sound nervous.

"Kiss me!" Kimberly said.

Sure enough, Gunnar leaned dutifully over and kissed her. Once their lips met, Kimberly pounced. Her arms slapped around him so tightly that she reminded me of a starfish prying open a clam. Except that Gunnar didn't resist. He kissed her right back, and they started making out. Apparently, Kimberly *was* going to have sex with Gunnar, someone she didn't even like. In fact, it looked like she was going to have sex with him there on the couch right in front of Trish and me. In any event, their frantic coupling ended what had to be the shortest game of Truth or Dare in history.

But it wasn't quite over for Trish. "My turn!" she said.

Gee, I thought, I wonder what her dare is going to be?

But I had had enough. I stood up from the couch, and Trish sort of fell off me with a clunk. It seemed like

I was always pushing her away from me, but that wasn't my problem, was it?

"What's wrong?" Trish said.

"Nothing," I said. "I just don't want to play."

"Oh."

"I think I want to go home."

"Oh."

I ignored her and turned to Gunnar, who was still on the couch playing tongue depressor with Kimberly. "Gunnar?" When he didn't look up or even seem to hear me, I said, "Gunnar! I want to go home!"

This finally got his attention. "Huh?"

"I want to go home now."

"What are you talkin' 'bout?"

"What part of 'I want to go home' don't you understand?" I took a step toward the door. "Now give me your keys. I'll drive."

"But—"

"But what?"

He scurried upright, and I tried to ignore the embarrassing bulge in the front of his pants. Then he jerked me into the kitchen. "Russ, what are you doing? You promised you'd do this for me!" I'd never seen him look so intent about anything, not even the weekend before when he'd blackmailed me into going out with Trish for a third time.

"I promised I'd go out with Trish," I whispered. "And I did. Three times." I looked back at her, huddled up on the couch like a dejected crab. Kimberly, meanwhile, wasn't consoling her friend. No, she was downing another shot of tequila. I felt bad I'd hurt Trish's feelings, but there wasn't much I could do about it now.

"No!" Gunnar said to me. "You went out with her two and a half times! The third date's not over yet!"

"Yeah?" I said. "Well, fucking her wasn't part of the deal!" I wasn't a guy who used profanity very often. But who did he think I was—Russel Middlebrook, Male Prostitute?

"Jesus, Russ!" Gunnar said. "Don't be a dick!"

He was accusing *me* of being a dick? After blackmailing me into this date, lying about what was involved, getting drunk on me, and now refusing to let me go home?

"I'm not being a dick," I said, not as calmly as I would have liked. "I just want to go home."

"Yeah? Well, we're not going home yet!" His eyes warned me not to cross him on this, but this was one lighthouse that I had no choice but to ignore.

"Gunnar, I'm not staying!"

"Fine!" he said. "Then you can walk!" We were out in the middle of nowhere, probably miles from the nearest phone. Plus, it was the middle of the night.

"Fine!" I said, and I started for the front door. This time it was no bluff. So I'd be stranded miles from home. Any place was better than this.

"Russel?" said a tiny, tremulous voice from behind. Trish. "What's wrong? Where are you going?"

"Home!" I said.

"Huh?" Kimberly said from the couch, her fogged-up eyes trying to make some sense of me.

"But why?" Trish said.

Did I owe her an explanation? It seemed like I did. But what could I say?

"It's not you," I said. "It's me. This was just a bad idea."

At this, Trish started to snivel. So much for my making things better.

"Jesus, Russ!" Gunnar said. "You are *such* a dick!"

"Just shut up!" I said.

"*You* shut up!"

"You son of a *bitch*!" Kimberly said. I don't think Kimberly had a clue what was going on. She was just reacting to Gunnar's and my raised voices, and to Trish's tears.

"I'm going!" I said.

"Fine!" Gunnar said. "Go! Get the hell out of here! While you're at it, you can go to hell!"

"Russel!" Trish said. "Wait!" But there was nothing I could say to her that would make it make sense, so I didn't wait.

"He's an asshole," I heard Kimberly say. "Let him go."

"But don't think this is the end!" Gunnar called after me. "I'll get you for this!"

I didn't listen to any more. I pushed open the door and stepped out into the cold dark night, the remnants of my ship all wrecked and unsalvageable on the rocky shoals behind me.

## CHAPTER TWELVE

At least I still had Kevin. He was the one I called when I finally found a pay phone over two hours later. I woke him up, but when I told him where I was and a little about what had happened, he immediately agreed to come and get me. (I called my parents too and told them not to worry—that Gunnar had had a flat tire on the way home, but that we'd called AAA.)

Forty minutes later, Kevin finally arrived in his parents' car. It was almost two in the morning.

"You okay?" he said once I'd climbed inside.

"Yeah," I said, but I wasn't okay, and he knew it.

I started to tell him what had happened, but I'd barely even begun when I burst out bawling.

"Hey," he said. "'Sokay." Then he held out his arms for me, and I buried myself against his chest.

I'd never cried in anyone's arms before, but I have to recommend it. It felt really good.

After that, I finally told the story of everything that had happened that night. He just listened, and when I was done, he told me that I'd done the right thing by leaving, and that I didn't have anything to be ashamed of by crying. Then he kept holding me and stroking my hair and telling me that everything would be all right.

"Thanks for coming," I whispered.

"Hey," he said. "We're a team, you and me. Don'tcha know I'd do anything for you?"

Like I said, at least I still had Kevin. I wasn't sure what I'd do if I ever lost him.

The following Monday, I had no one to sit with at lunch. Min still wasn't talking to me, and I sure as hell wasn't sitting with Gunnar. So I sat with the Jocks. Now that I was a member of the baseball team, this seemed perfectly normal. But, of course, I made a point of not sitting right next to Kevin.

"'Sup, Middlebrook?" Ramone said to me, and I nodded my hello. My star had faded a bit since I'd hit that winning home run over a week ago, but people still acknowledged my existence.

"Then what happened?" Nolan was saying to Jarred. I'd interrupted a conversation in progress.

"What do you *think*?" Jarred said. "Man, she was *begging* for it, squirming around like a baby!"

"Yeah?" Nolan said.

"Oh yeah!" Jarred said. "And then once I started going at her, she couldn't get enough. She was begging me for more!"

That's a lot of begging, I thought. Who was Jarred dating—a homeless person? But ever since I'd joined the baseball team, I'd known that if I was going to spend a lot of time with jocks, I was going to spend a lot of time listening to them brag about sex, especially on Mondays. For some reason, all the sex talk had been easier to stomach before Kevin and I had got together. Now that I had some idea what real intimacy was, it just made the guys sound like idiots, and cruel idiots at that. I glanced over at Kevin, but he was staring down at his food, which I took to mean that he was thinking the same thing.

Before Jarred could say any more, a hush swept over the lunchroom. I immediately knew what had happened. The lunchroom crowd reacted this way for one reason and one reason only. Someone had done something to Brian Bund.

I turned to where everyone was looking.

Sure enough, there was Brian Bund standing by a pair of double doors that led into the darkened school theater. Someone on the other side of those double doors had just pushed him out into the cafeteria. That wasn't all they'd done. They'd also wrapped a bra tightly around his chest, then smeared lipstick and rouge all over his face.

A nanosecond later, the lunchroom exploded in laughter. The thunderous roar hit him like a wave, and Brian actually stumbled backward a little.

I scanned the lunchroom. Once again, it seemed like almost everyone was laughing—from the Guy Jocks to the Computer Geeks. A few of the laughs looked a little forced, but most people looked like they really were busting a gut. I couldn't help but notice that Terese, sitting with the Girl Jocks, was laughing. There were two adult lunchroom monitors, and even one of them was smiling a little.

But then I spotted Min, sitting with her other friends. She wasn't laughing. Belinda and Ike were sitting with their friends too, but neither of them was laughing. I looked for Kevin's reaction, but Ramone was in my way, and I couldn't tell if Kevin was laughing or not.

Meanwhile, Brian panicked. This was too much, even for him. Unlike that time when people had thrown food at him, he didn't walk slowly for the door, steady and dignified. No, this time, he clawed desperately at the bra around his chest, finally managing to tear it off, even though it had obviously been tied tightly in back. Then, throwing the bra to one side, he went racing for the bathroom where he could wash off the lipstick and rouge. And while the makeup was thick, it couldn't cover the terror on his face. He looked like a tortured four-year-old, and I wondered how anyone could possibly find that expression funny.

A second later, Nate Klane and Brent Ragell rounded a corner into the cafeteria. They were both jocks—Nate was even a member of the baseball team. And maybe it was the way they were walking (an even cockier swagger than usual), but somehow I knew they'd just come from inside that darkened theater. They'd done their stuff to Brian, pushed him out into the lunchroom, then exited out a back door. Now they were pretending—barely—that they didn't know what had happened.

No one in the cafeteria was buying it. They knew Brent, they knew Nate, and they knew what they had done. The laughter got louder still—I almost expected people to start applauding—and Brent and Nate acknowledged their deed with little smirks and tiny little bows.

I doubted they'd get in trouble for their actions. Maybe they'd acted alone in this, but they hadn't really been alone. They'd been acting for the whole school. That's why no one, not even Brian, would tell on them. Besides, they were jocks. Jocks got special treatment. And as long as I ate lunch with them, I'd get special treatment too.

Funny thing, though. Even though I was sitting at a table jammed with people, I suddenly felt almost completely alone.

The next day, at the meeting of the Geography Club, the air was so cold you could have carved ice sculptures. There was Ike's ongoing resentment of me. And Min and Terese, who normally giggled and whispered before the start of every meeting and who held hands during the meeting itself, weren't even looking at each other. (Had they had a fight? Since Min was no longer speaking to me, I didn't know.)

Even Belinda seemed cool toward everyone.

It didn't help that Min brought up the subject of Brian Bund again right off the bat. We'd had a pep rally the previous Thursday, so this was our first meeting since the Tuesday before, when we'd last argued about Brian.

"Everyone saw what happened to Brian yesterday in the lunchroom," Min said.

"Yeah," Kevin said. "So?"

"So you still think we shouldn't let him in the Geography Club?"

"We talked about this last week," Terese said, sounding irritated.

"So?" Min said. "I want to discuss it again."

"There's nothing to discuss," Kevin said. "We already had a vote."

"Then I'll use my five minutes."

Nobody could argue with that. During your five minutes, you were supposed to be able to say anything you wanted, and no one could interrupt.

So for five minutes, Min told us again how she thought we should invite Brian to join our club. I won't say everything she said because, frankly, we'd covered all the arguments the week before.

When she was done, we were silent for a second.

Then Terese said, "Okay. Who's up next?"

"Wait a minute!" Min said. "I want another vote."

"We already voted," Kevin said. "Last week."

"So? There's no rule we can't have another vote."

"Yeah, well, you already had your five minutes. It's somebody else's turn."

"Yeah?" Belinda said. "Well, now it's *my* turn, and I think we should have another vote too."

"That's not fair," Kevin said.

"Let's just have another goddamn vote!" Terese shouted. That shut everyone up.

Kevin sighed. "Look, we all know what we're talkin' about. Anyone wanna change their vote from last week?"

Min looked at Terese hopefully. "Terese?"

*"Min!"* Terese said through clenched teeth. "We talked about this, okay?" That's when I knew they had been fighting, and that Brian had factored into it big-time.

When Terese said this, Min got the saddest look in her eyes, like she'd just seen a mother watch her own baby die. I knew then and there that Terese and Min were finished. This thing about Brian had been a jigsaw tearing through their relationship.

"Anyone else?" Min said, and I desperately tried to avoid her gaze.

No one said anything for a second. Then Ike said, "I do."

"You do what?" Terese said.

"Want to change my vote," Ike said. "I think we should ask Brian to join the club."

"What?" Kevin said. "Why?"

Ike shrugged. "I guess it was seeing him in the lunchroom yesterday. I mean, everyone has a breaking point. Well, Brian's got to be getting pretty close to his. So what if he went and did something extreme? I'd feel really bad knowing we could've done something to help him, but we didn't."

No one said anything, but we all knew what Ike meant. What if Brian killed himself? Coming from Ike especially, this was pretty powerful stuff. Once again, I'd been wrong about Ike. I never in a million years expected him to change his vote on this. But even though I knew he was doing the right thing and everything, I also hated him more than ever right then. Because with Ike voting with Min and Belinda, that meant the vote was now three to two. If I voted with Kevin and Terese, then the vote was three to three, and

187

we still wouldn't ask Brian to join the Geography Club, just like Kevin wanted. But if I changed my vote too, then the vote was two to four, and Min would get her way. In other words, my vote wasn't symbolic anymore. Suddenly, it mattered. Thanks to Ike, I was now the deciding vote!

"Russel?" Min said, with guarded optimism in her voice. She knew how close she was to winning this argument, and I knew that all would be forgiven if only I voted her way. And even as annoyed with Min as I was, I still thought she was right about Brian Bund, and I really did want to vote her way. But then I saw her and Terese sitting there stiffly, not talking, not touching. I thought, Is that what will happen to Kevin and me if I vote against him? It seemed impossible that we could break up over such a stupid issue. But it had been enough to drive Min and Terese apart, hadn't it?

I knew I couldn't handle not having Kevin to talk to and hold. We were a team, him and me. He'd said so himself. I couldn't stand being alone again.

And so I sold Brian Bund out for a third time. (The same number of times the apostle Peter denied Jesus Christ, in case you're interested.)

"I'm sorry," I said, eyes downcast. "No."

For a second, Min just sat there, stunned. Then

suddenly, she bolted upright. "Fine!" she said, seeth-ing. With that, she started for the door. It was pretty clear she was never coming back.

I could have stopped her. At any point before she reached that door, I could have piped up and said I'd change my vote, and she would have stopped. But who knows how Kevin would have reacted to that? It was a no-win situation.

So while I could have stopped Min, I didn't. She disappeared out into the hallway.

"Min!" Belinda said. "Wait!" When Min didn't reappear, Belinda hurried after her.

After that, Terese said, "Screw it!" And without so much as a good-bye, Terese followed them out.

That left Ike, Kevin, and me. We didn't even have a quorum.

The three of us didn't say anything. We didn't have to. We all knew what had happened. The Geography Club had come undone.

That afternoon at baseball practice, I struck out. Four times. The harder I swung the bat, the faster the ball seemed to whiz by me at the plate. This was a metaphor for something, and I was pretty sure what it was.

The truth was, I hadn't had any home runs since that first game eleven days before (I hadn't even had that many *hits*), and people were starting to notice. My fielding was better, but only a little. I wasn't absolutely the worst player on the team—that was Christian Coles—but I was definitely in the bottom third.

Kevin and I hadn't said anything to each other all practice long, but this wasn't strange. We usually made a point not to act too chummy at practice. What was different was that after that meeting of the Geography Club, I didn't particularly *want* to talk to him. This was ironic; I'd voted against Brian so Kevin wouldn't be mad at me, and now here I was, mad at him.

Afterward, he caught up with me on the way to the locker room. "Russel?" he said. "You okay?"

"Yeah," I said, and kept walking.

"Hey," he said, and I stopped, but I didn't look his way. He looked around for a place where we could talk in private, then finally led me into the trees behind the bleachers.

"What's goin' on?" he said. He was flipping a baseball in his hand. He was nervous about something, but I'd never known him to do that with just me before.

"Nothing," I said.

"I know it sucks not being in the starting lineup," he said. "But you'll get better. You're just havin' a bad week."

"It's not that," I said. "I couldn't care less about that."

He nodded once and looked away. "I know. It's that thing with Brian." So Kevin knew what was going on after all. "You think we should've let him into the club. You only voted the way you did because you thought that's how I wanted you to vote. Didn't you?"

Yeah, I thought bitterly. And now you've made me choose between you and my best friend. But all I said to Kevin was, "It's no biggie." I turned to go. "We should get back to the locker room before anyone notices we're gone."

"Wait," he said.

I stopped and looked back at him. He hadn't stopped flipping that baseball into the air.

"I think you should vote the way you want," he said. "For Brian, I mean."

"It's too late," I said.

"No, it's not. You can tell Min you changed your mind. I'm sure she'll come back to the Geography Club if you tell her that. And maybe we can talk Terese into coming back too. Then everything'll be just like before. I mean, except we'll have Brian as a member."

"And you'll stay a member too?" I said.

He nodded and grinned his famously dimpled grin. "Yeah. I'll stay a member too."

"Thanks!" I said, and before I could stop myself, I stepped forward and kissed him.

But my lips had barely touched his when he pulled away. "We should get back," he mumbled. And as he turned away, I couldn't help but notice that he was still flipping that baseball into the air, even faster than before.

The next morning before classes, I ran into Jarred Gasner on my way into school.

"Hey," I said.

When Jarred didn't answer, I looked over at him. He was staring at me with a funny expression. Cold almost.

*"What?"* I said. I knew I didn't have any zits. Did I have a booger hanging out of my nose or something?

"Is it true?" he said.

"Is what true?" I said.

"That you're a fag."

I felt my blood flash-freeze.

*"What?"* I said. "Who told you that?"

"Everyone," Jarred said. "Everyone's sayin' it. That you're the gay kid Toles was talking about. And that yesterday you turned in an application to start some kind of faggot club."

"No!" I said. *"No!"* I wasn't sure if I was talking to Jarred or the universe at large.

I was stunned. Who in the world would make up a lie like this? But even as I thought this, I knew the answer.

It was Gunnar's idea of revenge!

# CHAPTER THIRTEEN

And so began the worst day of my life. Suddenly, I was The Gay Kid. I don't think of myself as a pessimistic person, but somehow this just figured. I'd wanted so badly for this *not* to happen that it had to happen eventually, if you know what I mean. I'd been a shit to Brian and Min, and I knew I deserved to be punished—but did it have to be this?

In a way, the day itself was like the first school day after I hit that home run. People I had never spoken to before whispered my name in the hallways. Groups of kids fell silent as I walked by. But, of course, people weren't noticing me in awe and admiration. Now they were looking at me with pity or contempt—mostly contempt. As for the teachers, they no longer had glints in their eyes when they talked to me; now they had little quivers of hesitation, like they were thinking, If I'm nice to The Gay Kid, will I be fired like Ms. Toles was?

At lunch that day, I *really* didn't have anyone to sit with. Obviously, Gunnar and the jocks were out, and I figured Min was still mad at me. I couldn't very well force myself on Belinda or Ike.

Then I noticed a table where one kid was sitting all by himself.

I approached him and said, "Hey."

Brian Bund looked up at me. "Hey," he said. He didn't seem surprised to see me, which actually offended me a little.

"Mind if I sit here?" I said.

"Sure, I g-g-g-guess." So Brian Bund stuttered. Never having spoken to him or been in a class with him, I hadn't known this. But it figured too. Pimples, scrawny body, *and* a stutter. Anyone who never doubted the existence of a just and merciful God had never met Brian Bund.

I took a seat. Over the past few weeks, I'd been exploring the Land of the Popular, and the Landscape of Love, but they weren't the only two places I'd visited.

I'd covered the whole terrain of a typical high school. I'd gone from the Borderlands of Respectability, to the Land of the Popular, and now to Outcast Island, also known as Brian's lunch table. I'd made the complete circuit. But Outcast Island was the end of the line. In the world of high school, you could go from Respectable to Popular, or from Popular to Respectable, but you couldn't go anywhere from Outcast. Once you were there, you were stuck. That was the whole point of being exiled from someplace: you couldn't ever go back. Brian Bund's lunch table was the one place I hadn't ever expected to visit, but I knew I had better get used to it. It was my new homeland, and I was here to stay.

"So," I said to Brian. "Here we are."

Brian just looked at me. I definitely needed a new conversation-starter.

"Look," I said. "I'm really sorry about the other day in the hallway." When he didn't seem to know what I was talking about, I said, "I was with some guys from the baseball team? We made fun of you?"

"Oh," he said. Apparently, that kind of thing happened to him so often that he didn't really remember the separate incidents.

"So," I said. "I guess you heard about me?"

"That you're g-g-g-gay? Yeah, I heard. Is it true?"

I nodded. "But not the part about me being the kid Toles was talking about in that newspaper article— the one who supposedly just turned in an application for a gay club. Someone made up a lie about me, and part of it just happened to be true."

Brian didn't say anything, just kept eating his lunch.

"Do you care?" I said.

"That you're g-g-g-gay?" he said, and when I nodded, he said, "That would make me some k-k-k-kind of hypoc-c-c-crite, wouldn't it?"

I smiled in spite of myself. So Brian Bund had a sense of humor. I guess he needed to, given everything he had to put up with.

"Are you?" I said. "Gay, I mean?" I hoped he wasn't offended by my asking, but after everything that had happened, I really wanted to know.

"No," he said. "I thought I was for about a w-w-week once. But now I know I'm not."

If there was ever an answer that sounded like the truth, that was it.

"How do you do it?" I said. I wasn't sure if he'd know that I was talking about his being an outcast, but he did know.

"You get used to it," he said simply.

"All day long, I've felt like I'm going to burst into tears. Everyone staring at me, whispering things."

"No. You c-c-c-can't think like that."

"What do you mean?"

"You can't c-c-care what people *think*. You'll go c-c-c-crazy. You've g-got to save your energy for when people really d-d-d-do stuff."

Do stuff? I thought. But even as I thought this, I knew what kind of stuff he meant. Stuff like throwing food at him in the cafeteria. Or pulling him into a darkened theater and dressing him up like a girl. Or trapping him in a deserted hallway after school.

It was good advice. It was also a fascinating insight into his life, even if it was phenomenally depressing.

"You ever want to change the way things are?" I said.

He looked down at his food. "Things don't change. Not for me, they d-d-d-don't." I didn't bother giving him some stupid pep talk about having a better attitude. He was absolutely right. For him, things never would change, not as long as he stayed at Goodkind High School. And now they wouldn't ever change for me either.

"Besides," Brian said, "it's too late to change

things now that I'm eating lunch with the g-g-g-gay kid."

I smiled and thought, If I have to be banished to Outcast Island for the rest of my high school days, there are worse people to be stuck here with than Brian Bund.

The one good thing about school days is that, no matter how crappy they are, they eventually have to come to an end.

I hadn't seen Kevin all day. I'd ditched third period P.E. (Twenty teenage boys with boxing gloves, dodge balls, and baseball bats? I was no fool.) I'd also missed Kevin at lunch.

But I knew the route he took to baseball practice went right by the school Dumpster, so I waited for him there. Of course, I hadn't counted on the garbage stinking to high heaven. I thought, What is it about my relationship with Kevin and bad smells? For the rest of my life, I'd probably get a hard-on every time I smelled rotten eggs.

Finally, Kevin appeared. He was alone, which meant we could talk, and I felt myself relax for the first time in six hours. I knew Kevin couldn't actually make everything all right, but he could make everything *feel* all right. After all, he'd done it twice before, after my second and third dates with Trish Baskin.

Kevin hadn't seen me standing by the Dumpster, so when he got closer, I said, "Hey."

He jumped a little in surprise. He had kind of a panicky expression on his face, but I couldn't really blame him for not looking happier to see me. I mean, it was a sticky situation for him, me now being an outcast and all. And we were basically right out in the open where anyone could see. Still, I'd been desperate for his smile, and I was disappointed when it didn't appear.

I made sure there still wasn't anyone around, then I said, "We don't have to talk now, but I really need to see you. Meet me at the stinky picnic gazebo tonight at nine."

Kevin still wasn't smiling. He wasn't saying anything either. He just stared at me with this weird blank expression.

"What?" I said, but I had a feeling what.

He glanced back toward the school. "I don't think I can make it," he said.

"What?" I said. "Why not?"

"I just can't."

"Tomorrow then."

"I can't then either," he said.

"What are you saying?" He definitely couldn't be telling me he didn't *ever* want to see me again. That wasn't possible. He and I were a *team*.

But at that exact moment, we heard voices coming from the direction of the main building. It was Nate Klane and Ramone Hernandez, two members of the baseball team, probably also on their way to practice.

Kevin jerked toward them. I knew he'd never forgive me if they saw us together, so I backed up and crouched down in the space between the Dumpster and a nearby wall. The stink was a lot stronger there, and I found myself squatting in a layer of sticky orange goo. There weren't really any shadows for me to hide in, but I doubted Nate and Ramone would notice me, not unless they happened to look right at me.

"Yo, Lando!" Nate said as he and Ramone approached. (Lando was one of Kevin's many nicknames. In case you're wondering, I didn't have any nicknames, and now I never would. Not the friendly kind anyway.)

"'Sup?" Kevin said. He sounded as nervous as I felt.

"What's goin' on?" Nate said. "Gonna do some Dumpster-diving?"

"Nothin'," Kevin said, quickly turning away from the garbage. "Come on, let's get to practice."

But Nate was just finishing eating an ice-cream bar. "Hold on," he said, turning for the Dumpster so he could throw away the stick.

I hope it comes as no surprise that he spotted me instantly.

"Middlebrook?" he said, confused. "What the hell?"

Of course, Kevin and Ramone turned to look.

"I . . . lost something," I said to Nate, and it sounded just as stupid as it reads. I crawled out of my hiding place and tried to stand up straight. There wasn't much else I could do to regain my dignity. It was buried somewhere deep inside that Dumpster.

"Jesus, Middlebrook," Nate said, as if I hadn't spoken at all. "What were you doin' back there? Waitin' for your boyfriend?"

Nate and Ramone laughed, and I thought, Nate, if you only knew how right you are. Kevin was laughing too, but I knew I couldn't be too upset by this. Just because I was now an outcast, that was no reason to take him down too. And so in public, Kevin needed to treat me like any other jock would—namely, like shit. I understood that.

"Either that, or he's lookin' for something to eat," Ramone said. "What about it, Middlebrook? Find any wieners?"

Nate and Ramone and Kevin laughed some more.

Finally, Kevin said, "He don't want a wiener—he wants a big ol' sausage!" As he said this, Kevin made this really wide gesture with his hands, the kind a fisherman makes when he's talking about a fish. There was finally a smile on Kevin's face, but it wasn't the one I'd been expecting. It was a cruel sneer, the kind that Brian Bund was usually on the receiving end of.

It was one thing for Kevin to do the treat-me-like-shit act, but did he have to do it so convincingly? Except that this was no act, and I knew it. Kevin was telling me he wasn't coming to the stinky picnic gazebo, tonight or ever. That's what he'd started to say before, when Nate and Ramone had arrived. Spending any time around me now was just too risky.

A lot of people might say I deserved to be treated the way Kevin was treating me. I'd learned something from all those novels in English class. This was an example of the main character—me—getting his comeuppance because of his hubris. (See? I even know the lingo.) Now I knew exactly what it had felt like for Brian Bund that afternoon in the hallway, when Jarred and Nolan and I had cornered him on the steps. But at least I, unlike Kevin, hadn't made fun of anyone for being gay.

"Come on," Nate said. "Let's get outta here." And he and Ramone and Kevin started walking away, like I was an inanimate object, like the Dumpster itself, not worthy of even the vaguest of good-bye nods.

"Cocksucker," I heard Nate mumble.

I stood there in the stink of all that garbage, and I knew that I was finally, really, completely alone.

## CHAPTER FOURTEEN

Needless to say, I didn't go to baseball practice. Instead, I went for a walk. Eventually, I ended up at the Children's Peace Park, that place where I'd come with Min, with the cheesy wooden cut-outs of the children of the world. But those cut-outs had been vandalized the last time I'd been here, and someone had finally taken them down. Now it was just a flower garden, with lots of tulips and azaleas and irises, all in full bloom. It reminded me of a cemetery, which seemed fitting somehow. It could have been a memorial for the death of the Geography Club. Or maybe just a remembrance garden for my worth as a human being.

"Hey," a voice said from behind me. It was Min.

Somehow that seemed fitting too.

I sensed her stepping up next to me, but I couldn't turn to face her. We both just stood there side by side, staring at the flowers.

"How'd you find me?" I said.

"You weren't at home. There weren't that many places you could be."

"Are you really talking to me again?"

"I'd have to be pretty low to ditch you now."

I didn't know what to say. I was afraid if I opened my mouth, I'd start crying.

"I saw Kevin with some jocks," I said at last. "He laughed at me."

"He was scared," Min said. "A lot of people have been scared lately."

This was a reference to me, to what I'd done to Brian. She was right, of course. What Kevin had done to me wasn't really any different from what I'd done to Brian. Min's saying it made me realize one other thing too. Even now, I was still thinking only of myself.

"I was a jerk," I said. "I'm so sorry. I really screwed everything up, didn't I? I guess I'm getting what I deserved."

"No one deserves this," Min said, so firmly it gave me chills. "No one."

"It's over between you and Terese," I said. "Isn't it?"

Out of the corner of my eye, I saw Min nod.

"That was my fault too, wasn't it?" I said. "If I hadn't made fun of Brian in the hallway—"

"It wasn't anyone's fault," Min said, just as firmly as before. "It had to end. It was only a matter of time. It wasn't real to begin with. You can't have a relationship hiding in a warehouse in the middle of the night. I didn't even know her. The Geography Club, the thing with Brian, that just made me see her clearly for the first time."

"Well, I'm still sorry."

She shrugged. "Someday this will all be over. Five years from now, we'll probably look back on this and laugh."

Did that mean we'd still be friends in five years? "I can't believe you're really forgiving me," I said. I felt incredibly grateful to Min, but I was frightened too, that I'd somehow misinterpreted her.

"Russel," she said, "people make mistakes. If there was no such thing as forgiveness, there wouldn't be any friendships left in the world."

I turned to face her. She looked at me too. I'd never thought of Min as beautiful before, but now I saw that she was. Someday I'd have to write a song about her face or paint a painting of it. But I knew I could never do it justice.

"Remember a couple of weeks ago when you said I was a decent person?" I said, and she nodded. "That was wrong. You're the decent person. You're the best person I know."

"If I'm such a great person," Min said, "how come I feel like shit?"

I couldn't help but laugh. Ironically, it also gave me hope. I felt like shit too. Did that mean I wasn't such a terrible person after all?

That night after dinner, I was lying on my bed staring at the ceiling when I heard a knock on my bedroom window. My heart swelled up for a second, because I was certain it was Kevin. But when I tore open the drapes, it was Gunnar's face I saw outside. I don't think I'd ever been so disappointed in my entire life.

"Go away," I said. I didn't open the window. I closed the drapes in his face.

I could hear him knocking on the window again. "Russ, please?" I could just barely hear his voice through the glass. "Please let me talk to you for just one second?"

"Go away!" I said, as loud as I could be without my parents hearing. (Needless to say, my parents don't come into this story much. But then, they don't come into my life much either.) Anyway, Gunnar would be coming into my bedroom over my dead body.

"It wasn't me!" he said through the window. "I didn't start that rumor! Russ, I swear!"

What's this? I thought.

"Please let me explain!" Gunnar said.

I opened the drapes again and unlocked the window. I was still furious, and if my bedroom had been on the second floor and Gunnar had climbed up a trellis or something, I might have considered pushing him backward. As it was, my room was on the ground floor, and he was standing in the bushes right outside.

"What?" I said. The tone in my voice said he had a hell of a lot of explaining to do.

Gunnar's eyes were even wider than usual. "It was Trish and Kimberly! Well, mostly Kimberly. She wanted to get back at you. She said you'd embarrassed Trish. So, the next morning she came up with the idea of telling everyone you're the gay kid."

I thought about this. Knowing Kimberly like I did, it didn't stretch the bounds of credibility.

Gunnar looked down at the ground. "Okay, that's kind of a lie."

*"What?"* I said, livid again.

"Look, I'm telling you the entire truth, okay? And the truth is, I didn't try to talk them out of it. I don't know if they would've listened, but they might've. I was mad at you, so I let them go through with it." He kind of whispered the rest: "Maybe I even encouraged them a little."

I started to say something snotty, but Gunnar interrupted me. "And even if I *had* tried to talk them out of it, you still have every reason to be mad at me. You did me a big, big favor by going out with Trish, and I paid you back by lying to you. I shouldn't have asked you in the first place. And I really shouldn't have asked you the second and third times. And I shouldn't have let you walk out alone that night at the beach place, or said the things that I said. And I am so sorry! Russ, you're my best friend, and I have never been this sorry about anything in my life!"

I couldn't help but remember what Min had said about friendships and forgiveness. But was this the kind of thing I could forgive? Was this the kind of thing I *should* forgive?

"It's true, you know," I said.

"What?" he said. He got some points for wiping away a tear.

"That I'm gay."

Gunnar rolled his eyes. "I know that."

"What? How long have you known?"

"Oh, maybe five years."

*"What?"* I could hardly believe my ears.

"Well, I'm not a complete idiot!" Gunnar said. "I mean, it's kind of obvious. Animated Disney musicals?"

"And do you care?"

"What?" he said. "That you're gay?" I nodded, and he said indignantly, "If I cared, would I be standing here with a juniper bush up my ass?"

"Why didn't you ever tell me you knew?" I asked.

"I figured you'd tell me when you got around to it. Anyway, the fact that I knew just makes it even shittier that I asked you to go out with Trish. I knew they probably wanted to fool around out at that beach place. I guess I also knew that Kimberly wouldn't go out with me unless you went out with Trish, just like you tried to tell me. All I can say is, sex, Russ. It made me go insane. That and the possibility that I might have a girlfriend for the first time in my life."

This is when something occurred to me. Gunnar had been doing the same kinds of crazy things to get together with Kimberly that I'd been doing to get together with Kevin. But rather than not caring about Brian Bund's feelings, he hadn't cared about mine. It was funny how everything was fitting together like this.

"So what happened?" I said. "Out at the beach place—after I left?"

He rolled his eyes again. "You'll be happy to know it was a complete disaster. Kimberly got sick all over the place, and Trish and I had to clean it up, even though I had a horrible hangover. And my mom was furious that I didn't come home that night—I'm grounded right now, by the way."

I took a breath, held it, and exhaled. Then I said, "Well, you better climb inside and tell me all about it." I had a lot to tell him too. In other words, I guess I'd decided to forgive the idiot after all.

I went to the stinky picnic gazebo that night at nine o'clock, just in case Kevin came after all—in case it really *had* been an act by the Dumpster after school, or in case he'd changed his mind since then. I was positive he wouldn't show.

I was right. He didn't.

## CHAPTER FIFTEEN

First thing at school the next morning, I ran into Jarred once again. I braced myself for another verbal blow.

Instead, he said, "Yo, man. Sorry about yesterday."

"What?" I said.

"'Bout calling you a fag and everything. I didn't believe it, but everyone was sayin' it, so I decided it must be true."

I was still sleeping, right? This was a dream. In a minute, Jarred would turn into a giant raspberry Popsicle.

"What made you decide it wasn't true?" I made myself ask.

"'Cause I saw the application. It's Brian. He's the one starting this whole fag club and shit. He's the one Toles was talking about. That's what I always thought anyway."

I considered asking Jarred some more questions, but then I decided I'd better shut up before I accidentally told him something I didn't want him to know.

I left Jarred and found Belinda in the hallway. "What's going on?" I asked.

"Oh!" she said, excited. "I've been looking for you! Last night, Brian came into the office to submit an application for a club. The Goodkind High School Gay-Straight Alliance! He's the only member. I tried to talk him out of it—he didn't even have a faculty advisor! What was the point of submitting an application for a club that was just going to be rejected anyway? But he was determined to do it, and he made me promise I'd turn it in. Finally, I did, and a couple other kids in the office took it, and now, well, everyone knows."

"So now everyone thinks Brian's The Gay Kid and not me?" I said, and Belinda nodded.

I finally found Brian sitting at a carrel hidden in the back of the library.

"Why?" I said.

He wouldn't look me in the eye, just kept staring at his book. "There's already one Brian Bund," he said simply. "There d-d-doesn't need to be one more."

So he'd submitted that application to clear my name, just like I'd thought. He'd probably even back-dated it a day, to make it look more like the rumor was true and that he was The Gay Kid, not me. He was sac-rificing himself in my place (just like You-Know-Who on the crucifix, or so some people think). How the hell did you repay someone for something like that?

"Thanks," I said, and boy, did I mean it. "People at this school have no idea what they're missing by not knowing you."

He nodded once and turned the page in his book.

I could hardly believe it. Maybe my story was going to have a happy ending after all!

That afternoon at lunch, Kevin met me just as I was leaving the buffet line. I had my lunch tray in my hands.

"Hey," he said. He wouldn't look me in the eye either.

"Hey," I said.

"Russel, I'm sorry. I'm *really* sorry."

"It's okay."

He looked up at me, trying to gauge whether or not I was telling the truth. "Really?"

"Yeah," I said. I knew I couldn't judge Kevin—not after the way I'd been acting the last few weeks. But it hurt to know that if I'd still been The Gay Kid—if Brian Bund hadn't agreed to take the fall for me—Kevin and I wouldn't be having this little reunion.

I looked around the lunchroom for a table. Min and Gunnar hadn't showed up yet.

"Sit with us," Kevin said.

"The jocks?" I said.

"Yeah. Everything's okay now."

"But yesterday I ate lunch with Brian. The Gay Kid. Don't people think that's strange?"

"I told everyone that was only because he was the only one who'd let you sit down. Because of what everyone else thought about you."

"Oh," I said. So Kevin had been in the lunchroom with me yesterday. He'd just been avoiding me. That figured.

"Come on," he said. "Let's sit."

I started to follow him to the Jocks table, but halfway there, I happened to glance across the room to Brian Bund, sitting by himself once again.

Suddenly, I knew how I could repay Brian for what he had done for me. How I *had* to repay him. Of course, I wanted to follow Kevin to the Jocks table. But I was being given a chance to redeem myself or whatever. On the subject of Brian Bund, I had three strikes, but I wasn't out yet. Incredibly, I was being given a fourth time at bat.

"Kevin," I said.

He stopped and turned to look at me.

"Go on ahead," I said. "I'm going to sit somewhere else."

"Huh?" He was confused.

"It's just that yesterday I made friends with Brian Bund."

"Yeah? Great."

"So he's a good guy."

Kevin still looked like he had no idea where I was going with this. "So?"

"So I'm going to *stay* friends with Brian Bund."

Kevin followed my gaze over to Brian's table. I could see the wheels in Kevin's head clicking into place as he realized what I was planning on doing.

He quickly stepped up alongside me. "Russel!" he whispered. "You really think that's a good idea?"

"Yeah. I think it's a great idea."

Kevin was still whispering. "But Russel. . . !" He didn't finish the sentence, but I knew what he was telling me. If I went through with this—if I actually sat down at Brian's table again—there'd be no turning back. This time, there were things I'd be giving up forever. My visa to the Land of the Popular, for one thing, and probably even my return ticket to the Borderlands of Respectability. But what Kevin didn't understand was that by sitting with Brian I was gaining something too, something I couldn't quite name, but that was more important than any of those things.

I just nodded at Kevin and said, "Go on ahead. I'll be okay."

Kevin didn't go on ahead. He watched me as I turned toward Brian's table and started working my way across the cafeteria. I knew that everyone else in that cafeteria was watching me too. The closer I got to Brian's table, the softer the rumble of voices became. By the time I reached him, there wasn't anyone talking at all. I knew what they were thinking, and it wasn't what they'd been thinking those days after I hit my first home run. But what did they know, right?

"Hey," I said to Brian. "Mind if I join you again?"

Brian looked up at me. This time, he did look surprised. But that didn't stop me from taking a seat.

## EPILOGUE

So you probably want to know if I ever saw Kevin again. That's what I wanted to know—if I ever *would* see him again, except passing me by in the hallways at school. But as a matter of fact, I did see him, the very night after My Big Moment in the cafeteria. He IMed me and told me to meet him at the stinky picnic gazebo. This being the epilogue, where everything is supposed to be all tied up nice and neat, I'd like to be able to say I didn't care what he had to say. But the truth was, I was dying to know what he had to say and, even now, I was desperately hoping he wanted to get back together with me, no matter what the terms.

He was already waiting there when I arrived, a

dark figure pacing back and forth with his hands in his pockets. When he saw me, he crossed the grass to where I was standing. We stood there awkwardly facing each other for a second. He'd been drinking, and I could smell the beer on his breath and clothing.

"Why?" he said. This was definitely the question of the day.

But I had a good answer for him. I explained to him about the application and how Brian had purposely turned it in with his name on it so people would think that he was the subject of the rumor, not me.

We just looked at each other. I knew what I wanted him to say. The question was, was he going to say it?

"You're a good guy," he said at last.

*But*, I thought.

He spun away from me. "Russel, I'm not that strong! The pressure—it's just too much! I *like* being popular!"

"I liked it too," I whispered. "I liked it a lot."

Suddenly, Kevin got an idea. "But we can still meet here, right? Everything can still be okay! I promise I won't bug you at school, and I'll make sure the other jocks don't either, and we can still come here and talk and be together, right?"

Everything froze. This was exactly what I had

wanted Kevin to say. So why wasn't I glad? A part of me *did* want everything to be okay. That part of me thought, Yeah, we *could* meet here every night to talk (and more), just like Min and Terese had done in their darkened warehouse on Fracton, and we could carry on like nothing had ever happened. But at the same time, another part of me knew that everything wasn't okay. We couldn't carry on like nothing had ever happened, because something *had* happened. A lot had happened, and it had changed the way I looked at him.

"Kevin. . . ," I said.

He nodded, his eyes heavy. "Yeah. I know that won't work. Russel, I'm sorry I let you down."

"It's okay," I said, and it really was. I'd forgiven another friend. But sometimes just because you forgive someone doesn't mean you still love them. This Landscape of Love was a very bizarre place. (Incidentally, I hope you didn't really think I was going to get back together with him. This *is* the epilogue, after all.)

He stepped forward and hugged me, and I felt his body, hard and lean and warm. In spite of everything, he still felt wonderful, like I was embracing a mountain. But I now knew that as solid as he seemed, he was no mountain.

He didn't pull away. I decided that had to be my

job. After all, I was the one who was ending it. (I was actually ending a relationship with *Kevin Land*?) I had to be the one who was strong.

When I did pull away, he started to shake and sob. But I kept pulling, and it felt like an amoeba separating—like half of my body was being torn away from me. But at the same time, it felt kind of good, like when you cut your fingernails too short, but you know they'll eventually grow back, cleaner and stronger than before.

"Good-bye, Russel," he said. It was weird to have the tears on his face for a change.

"Good-bye, Kevin," I said. Then I turned and starting walking away.

I'd like to say I didn't look back, but I did.

I think I always will.

As for me and everyone else, three weeks later, I was back in Kephart's classroom after school. But it wasn't for a meeting of the Geography Club.

"The Goodkind High School Gay-Straight Alliance," I said, trying out the new name of the group gathered around me. "Well, *that* has a terrifying ring to it!"

"Gay-Straight-*Bisexual* Alliance," Min corrected.

"Is everyone absolutely sure they want to go through with this?" I asked.

"Yup," Belinda said.

"Positive," Ike said.

"I'm in," Gunnar said.

"Me too," said Brian.

And Min just nodded and smiled at me reassuringly. "It's a gay-*straight* alliance," she said. "If anyone asks, we just say that a lot of our members are straight, which they are. We don't have to say which ones."

"Gay-straight-*bisexual* alliance," I reminded her.

Min giggled. "Touché."

Ever since I'd started sitting with Brian at lunch three weeks before, I'd been called my share of names, and I was definitely on the outs with the jocks (and Kevin). But incredibly, people still didn't think of me as gay. Brian was The Gay Kid (even if he wasn't really gay), and I was just being nice to him. I guess people couldn't quite grasp the fact that at a school of eight hundred students, there might actually be more than one gay kid. I couldn't complain; just a couple months before, I'd thought there could only be one gay kid (me!). Besides, now for the first time in my life, homophobic ignorance was working to my advantage.

But all that was about to change. None of the six of us gathered in Kephart's classroom—Min, Gunnar, Belinda, Ike, Brian, and me—had any idea what would happen when the teachers and other students found out about the Goodkind High School Gay-Straight-Bisexual Alliance. Would we be banished to Outcast Island? Or would we maybe, just maybe, be allowed to stay in the Borderlands of Respectability? (Let's face it: the Land of the Popular was no longer an option.)

I didn't care. None of us did. Because wherever we ended up, we'd be there together. And I now knew that even the ugliest place in the world can be wonderful if you're there with good friends—just like the most fabulous destination on earth is pretty boring when you're all alone. And when it came to friends, you couldn't ask for better ones than Min, Belinda, Brian, and yes, even Ike and Gunnar.

Now that we were going public, maybe we'd even be joined by the "real" Gay Kid—the kid Ms. Toles had been talking about in the newspaper article that had started all this in the first place. Maybe there were other kids at our school who would join us too.

"So what do we d-d-d-do now?" Brian said.

I explained that with the Geography Club, we had gone around in a circle, with everyone getting five minutes to say whatever they wanted.

"Who wants to go first?" Belinda said. "Russel?"

"Someone else go," I said. For the first time in my life, for the time being at least, I'd already said everything I had to say.